SECRET SANTA

Jade is a journalist, attached to her boyfriend, Brad, but impossibly drawn to photographer Carl. With Christmas approaching, an exotic Secret Santa gift at work confuses her further, but why does Carl run a mile whenever the heat starts to sizzle between them? Family problems add to Jade's seasonal blues — can she find contentment before the big day arrives . . . ?

JULIE GOODALL

SECRET SANTA

Complete and Unabridged

LINFORD
Leicester

First published in Great Britain

First Linford Edition
published 2014

A catalogue record for this book is available
from the British Library.

ISBN 978–1–4448–1863–5

Published by
F. A. Thorpe (Publishing)
Anstey, Leicestershire

Set by Words & Graphics Ltd.
Anstey, Leicestershire
Printed and bound in Great Britain by
T. J. International Ltd., Padstow, Cornwall

This book is printed on acid-free paper

1

' 'tis the season to be jolly, tra la la la la la la la la.' The age-old song crackled out of someone's computer, but Jade did her best to tune it out. Jolly was not how she felt, with Brad leaving early tomorrow on an assignment and Christmas music and lights filling all of the shops.

The office buzzed with joviality and heightening spirits, but as the week preceding Christmas Eve approached, Jade was only ever reminded of the heightening tension in her home all those years ago, the increase in frequency and intensity of the arguments, ending in her father's admission of adultery. The slam of the door as he left mid evening, the night before Christmas, took along with him Jade Cooke's belief in all things magical. She had soon learned there were some things even Santa couldn't make right.

'Jade? Jade!'

She looked up from her desk, surprised to discover all eyes were upon her.

Sara Maxwell from advertising stood at the front of the office, Secret Santa presents piled high on the chair beside her, although not quite as high as the hem of her skirt.

For a moment, Jade took in the golden brown of Sara's thighs, almost convinced by their authenticity had she not seen the fake tan poking out from her bag back in October. Not that many guys tapping away behind their desks here cared two hoots about that, she thought wryly, rising from her behind her own desk with slow deliberation. If it looked good, it looked good, no matter the means of getting it. Kayleigh Oswald in accounts had new boobs for her twenty-fifth birthday — the attention she'd received since was a firm testament to that.

And what would it be this year? she wondered, weaving up the aisle, remembering what most of the girls got in their parcels twelve months ago. Perfume? Chocolates? Jewellery? A voucher for one of the trendy fashion stores?

She accepted the parcel with grace and a smile more real than the one she received from Miss Maxwell, and was immediately aware of the reason.

Jade could feel Brad Wilson's eyes were upon her, despite Sara's best attempts to divert them, and Jade knew Sara would up the ante at any given opportunity to deflect attention from Brad Wilson's girlfriend to herself.

Turning away, Jade caught his eye and received a wink that would have turned Sara's envy to green jelly. His tan was straight from the heat of Mauritius, more than a match for Sara's bottle from Boots, and she looked forward to feeling the smoothness of it under her palms later that night.

He'd been back from the stag week for over five weeks now and, at first, she had laughed at his insistence on moisturising his skin when he got back, but she'd quite gotten into it. The administering of the moisturiser had rather quickly turned into an erotic massage routine and, inevitably, once every inch of his bronzed skin glistened with lotion, the attention had turned to herself. If only it hadn't been quite so short-lived.

Nevertheless, the memory flamed desire through her veins, heat seeping from them into her skin and she returned Brad's wink with a smile of satisfaction, gathered herself into the present then forced a nonchalant stride back to her desk.

The room buzzed with chatter and the rip of paper exposing the gifts beneath. Strips of sellotape made access to her own present laborious, but finally she peeled back the folds of paper to reveal a quite decent bundle of nail varnish along with a manicure set.

It seemed a real girly present and she glanced around furtively, wondering which colleague had drawn her name from the oh-so-classy plastic bowl kept for such an occasion in the cupboard under the printers. Mandy on Health? Yasmin from HR? It wasn't Sara, that was for certain. Sara would have bought Jade something sure to increase her weight or make her breath smell.

Jade had barely eased the blue varnish out of its plastic carton when Sara's voice pierced into the room once again.

'Erm, there seems to be one over. Hold on, everyone . . . ' She held a perfectly manicured finger aloft, revelling in the attention. 'Let's see, it's for . . . ' This time her voice was slightly disconsolate as she held up a large rectangular parcel wrapped in glossy black paper with silver stars. A ribbon ran the length and the width of it, blooming into a blood red rose in the centre. 'Jade Cooke. Again. I don't know what's happened here.' Her tone dropped into a canyon of disgust but was barely noticeable as every gaze in the room swung back to Jade.

'Another one, for me? Are you . . . ?' Jade knew better than to question Sara

Maxwell, leaving the last word unsaid.

Fighting the surprise attempting to pin her to her seat, she quickly returned to the front of the room. The parcel was thrust upon her and she took it without comment or thanks. Her desk was becoming cluttered and, when back to it, she moved all else aside, intrigued by this new and elaborate development.

She sensed she wasn't alone as some people had moved from their desks, closer to hers and, from the corner of her eye, she saw Brad rise from his seat and ease himself nearer, loitering in the background.

No other offering had possessed such sophistication, such size or been quite so decorative and, unused to being the centre of attention, Jade's fingers quivered a little as they tussled with the undressing of the gift.

Beneath the wrapping lay a large white box, unsealed, so her access was now unimpeded and, inside, pure white tissue paper shrouded something delicate and light.

As she peeled back the tissue, her fingertips met with pink and black lace and, soon, the whole office was witness to the revelation of a pair of lacy black knickers with pink ribbon ties for each hip. On delving into the tissue, another item showed itself to be a matching bra with lacy pink trim, reflecting the colour now spreading over Jade's chest, racing up her neck and onto her cheeks.

A rumble moaned through the room, along with the odd wolf whistle and, instinctively, Jade's gaze sought out Brad amongst the bodies around her. Somehow she didn't think this particular gift was from one of her female colleagues and a glance at the label had told her the size was correct.

This additional Secret Santa had to be him and a rush of hope flashed through her. Perhaps he had also realised that things were not as they once were.

'Not quite what I was expecting,' she managed, catching the back of Sara's head from behind Brad as she moved away as if repelled.

Brad's turquoise eyes flashed at her with a glint of amusement and Jade's flush deepened as she rewrapped the lingerie in the tissue and placed it into her bag.

'Better recycle the box,' she muttered, thankful for an excuse to break through the throng now surrounding her desk.

By the time she returned from the cardboard recycle bin, colleagues were filtering slowly back to their workstations, interest now apparently lessened in the gifts they had received.

Brad was lounging beside her monitor, one hand playing with her mouse whilst the other rested on the back of her chair. When Jade took her seat, he failed to move but remained right in her space and, as he bent over to whisper in her ear, she could feel the heat of him warming the air between them. The familiar woodiness of his aftershave stirred memories from when he'd returned from the stag week and she found herself wishing again that she could turn the clock back.

'A bit more interesting than what I got,' he confessed, a movement in his arm flexing the hard line of his muscle. 'A snowman globe with a misplaced carrot. Not that yours would have suited me much.'

Jade laughed aloud at the thought.

'Might be quite fun to try it,' she returned suggestively, searching the angular features on his face. 'Me, I mean,' she added, in case he misread her. 'So, when did you find time to buy those?' she asked, feigning innocence, but he refused to give anything away.

'Who said I did?' His finger moved lazily over the wheel of the mouse, sending the cursor on Jade's screen into a spin. 'It's *Secret* Santa. Remember?'

The electric blue of his eyes seemed to send out a signal, but Jade felt at a loss to read his surreptitious code. The next moment, the heat of him had vanished leaving the air around her chilled, the mouse abandoned, her cursor perfectly still.

Willing herself not to and failing, she

glanced behind her, watching the tightness of Brad's backside disappear in the direction of either advertising or accounts.

Turning back, still on the screen was the piece she had been working on before all the furore, based on a girl who had been knocked down on a zebra crossing in town.

The face of Daniel, her twelve-year-old brother, looked up at her from her desk and she retrieved the photograph from where Brad must have accidently knocked it from the side of her monitor. The blue tack remained sticky and she pushed it hard against the plastic to ensure it wouldn't dislodge again.

'Hey!'

Jade looked up at the inescapable squeak from Mandy.

With one last glance at the photo, she straightened, giving her colleague her full attention, guessing what would come next.

'Hi, Mandy. So, what did you get?'

'My favourite perfume, well, bodyspray.

You can't really expect someone in here to shell out seventy odd quid for some Chanel, although it would be nice, of course. I got make-up as well in the same box, Selfridges stuff, very nice, definitely my colours.' Her words tumbled over each other in the same way that her wayward curls always tumbled out of their clips and her laugh tinkled uncertainly into the office.

Jade smiled, remembering how she had peeked into Mandy's desk drawer last week to discover which bodyspray she used. She'd almost been caught out and had asked to borrow her stapler, at the same time trying to memorise the name of the spray she'd need to buy next time she was in town.

'Jade?' Mandy went on, glancing around as if to ensure no one was listening. 'I was thinking . . . well, do you think it could be him? I think it could,' she went on, not even waiting for a reply. 'I mean, he notices things, doesn't he? I think it's him. It must be.'

'Him?' Jade interrupted, pretending

stupidity, knowing full well who Mandy meant. Most of the office had lived through Mandy's obsession with Carl Heaney, the photographer on the Observer, and it had been a topic of conversation some moons ago, but the gossips had long since moved on.

She was hopeless at playing it cool, her tongue in fifth gear without her brain ever escaping neutral if he so much as approached where she sat. Her desk was just across the aisle from his, so she spent half her working day gazing at his profile whilst pretending to research articles on health. She was both terrified and fanatical — not a combination Jade ever found particularly turned a guy on.

'Carl!' the twenty-one-year-old whispered excitedly, drawing attention from John in the next cubicle, and suddenly Jade felt so much more than three years Mandy's senior. Somehow, a conversation with her colleague always felt like one she'd have had back at school. 'Those eyes could kill at ten paces and the way he looks at me . . . but I just don't get it. When I make an advance, he retreats like the Spanish Armada. D'you think he's just shy?'

The eventual pause for breath gave Jade a moment to think. Was Carl Heaney shy, she wondered, scrunching up the wrapping from her presents and tossing it into her bin? She looked around the room and found him by the Xerox, sorting sheets into piles. He cut a fine figure, with firm, masculine lines and arms like steel beneath long, white, shirt sleeves, exuding strength without effort. His backside gave Brad's a run for its money and there really was something about him that she couldn't quite put her finger on. He wasn't a massive flirter and didn't join in much with the lads in the office, although he still knew how to have a bit of a laugh.

At first glance, he seemed like the moderate type, but Jade had seen something flicker in the depth of his eyes on more than one occasion, making her wonder if 'moderation in all things' might not truly describe Carl Heaney at all.

Jade looked away quickly, concerned that her thoughts might give her away. Despite her best efforts, she couldn't help but recall how impressively Carl held her gaze when engaged in a conversation and it was almost as if, when they spoke, she'd hold her breath till it came to an end.

No, she decided, dragging her attention back to Mandy . . . when it came to Carl Heaney, shy wasn't a word that sprang straight to mind.

Surprised at how hard she found it to free herself from his image, Jade distracted herself with organising her new bottles of nail varnish, lining them up in front of her in-tray like multi-coloured soldiers. Strangely, the military image forced her gaze back to the Xerox and she found herself following Carl's trail back to his desk.

'He might be a bit shy,' she reassured, aware that Mandy was watching her, waiting for a reply. 'I think you should spray a bit on. You know, sort of show that you're interested. Then, if it is him, he might notice.'

Mandy was gone before Jade had time to look round. Within moments, a delicate floral odour drifted above the cubicles and Jade resisted the urge to cough.

Relieved when it had begun to dissipate, she smiled secretly at Mandy's exuberance, then sat and clicked the mouse to return to her screen.

She really should get on with this article. There'd been enough distractions and she had two more pieces to get done by the end of the day.

Drawing her chair up to her desk, she settled into work mode, beginning a reread of what she'd written so far. It was great human interest — teenager gets knocked down at night on a crossing, driver stops and gets out, then panics and drives off. One witness to the incident, boy's mate from college. No number plate taken — a loose, shocked description. Mate calls 999 and distraught parents call for information to be given to police. Drama, tragedy, unsolved crime.

The look in the boy's parents' eyes had broken Jade's heart as she'd interviewed them in their home.

'I'm glad I don't suffer from asthma.' The Irish lilt filtered gently into Jade's consciousness, breaking through the wall of concentration she had only just begun to construct.

The hairs on her arms rose at the sound of him and a smile broke the tightness of her lips as her intensity quickly dissolved. His breath was warm on her neck and she closed her eyes momentarily before attempting to gain her composure.

Carl Heaney's musky scent made her thankful she was already sitting down.

2

As Jade's gaze left the screen, she realised she'd sensed a presence before any words had been spoken and she turned into it, welcoming the power Carl's closeness had on her own breathing. Its pattern had swiftly changed from rhythmic and slow to shallow and fast, and it was stifling but she liked it.

'Do you have a mask in your drawer I could borrow?' he went on, leaning closer, ironically sucking the oxygen from her air.

'Oh, bless her, she's just excited,' Jade replied, with a coolness she didn't feel.

'A permanent condition for our Mandy, I fear.' Carl laughed, the deepness of it vibrating in the atmosphere between them, enveloping her with its warmth. She loved the sound of it, heartfelt and real.

'May I?'

He tapped the desk on the right of her chair and she nodded that he may as he settled his neat backside onto it.

Now that he was in front of her, she could fully take in the sight of him; solid, muscular shoulders and chest thinning down to lean hips; firm, thick thighs beneath his chinos. He was a tough, heavy-duty male and thoughts swept through her flustered brain that would have matched well with the lingerie sitting close by.

To be held by such a powerful body would surely be nothing but bliss, and she could sense the strength of him in his aura . . . a strength that made her feel wonderfully weak.

Jade could only imagine the sensual touch of the hands that were gripping the edge of her desk and fingering the photo of her brother on the monitor, and she battled the urge to reach out and brush one of his fingers as if by accident as she reached across for something she didn't need. Just to see. Just to know what it felt like. There was no way, she was sure, that a touch of his hand could affect her the way her imagination insisted, but she'd love to find out.

She continued to watch him in silence, curious as to the thoughts inside his head, noticing he was looking straight at the photograph and actually seeing it in a way that so many workmates didn't.

'How's your brother doing? Dan, isn't it?' He turned the photo a little bit more towards him then turned towards Jade. 'He wasn't so good last time we spoke.'

About three and a half weeks ago, Jade mentally reckoned . . . their last lengthy conversation. Not that she had been counting, but her chats with Carl stayed with her in a way that other chats in the office just didn't.

He usually talked about something, rather than the usual clichéd male conversation about sex or sport. Although sometimes she thought he may as well talk about sex as that's where her mind tended to drift whenever Carl Heaney came by for a chat.

Dan, she admonished herself, bringing her thoughts back as she focused on the photo instead of the fathomlessly deep brown eyes that were focused on her as she sat there. She shouldn't be thinking like this. She was with Brad Wilson, end of story. He might have his flaws, with his obsessions and domesticity, but she was far from perfect herself. She forced herself not to reach over for the photo, not to lean on the sturdy thigh so close to her arm.

'Well, to be honest, Carl, still not so good.' She drew herself back to his question. 'His behaviour has worsened a little lately, which makes things hard for Mum.'

For a moment her glance fell to her lap as she realised how hard it had been making life for herself too. Brad had recently been more reluctant than ever to visit her family home but, in truth, someone like Brad was never going to cope well with a disease like muscular dystrophy. He'd not been faced with anything like it in his life and the idea of illness — any illness — grossed him out.

Carl leaned closer, lowering his voice to an intimacy that would have made Jade perspire had the subject not been her beloved younger brother, and she responded in kind, unwilling to share such private matters with others around them.

She had spoken about Dan with Carl often and trusted his discretion implicitly. It was good, in fact, to be able to talk about Dan so openly with someone who wasn't family and not so emotionally involved.

'Dan's adapted to the wheelchair surprisingly well,' she admitted, 'which is quite a relief. The worry now is that his upper strength is going. At least at the moment he can move around in his chair on his own. Eventually, though . . .'

Jade's voice drifted off and she found herself unable to finish, but there was no need. She could see Carl knew what she was saying and they sat quietly for a while, amongst the office buzz all around them, staring at the twelve-year-old boy in the photo, blue-tacked into Jade's work-life.

Carl's sigh was subterranean as he stirred on the desk.

'I love sitting here,' he announced, faintly. 'It's my favourite place in the whole office.' He paused for a moment, seeming unsure whether to go on and Jade waited, her breath caught in her throat. 'The view is tremendous,' he continued, his gaze fixed firmly on hers. 'I really could sit here all day.'

Jade swallowed tightly, acutely aware that he wasn't looking around the office and finding it hard to tear her own gaze away. Finally, Carl lifted his broad shoulders in a fatalistic shrug and blew out a breath.

'Ah well. Guess I should get myself back to work before the boss does it for me.'

Leaning forwards once more into her

22

personal space, the moment hung, suspended, and she sensed that both wanted the moment to last, but Carl glanced towards the Editor's office then lifted an eyebrow.

Jade turned to see Jenny Jackson, Newspaper Editor, apparently on the warpath. Obviously the Christmas festivities had gone far enough for today.

'Jade and Carl!'

'Uh oh,' Jade giggled, catching Carl's glance of amusement, her hand tightening into a fist at the power of the shared moment. The names sounded somehow right together, sending a chill of delight up her spine. 'We're in trouble . . . '

'Someone's come along and they've burst our bubble,' he finished swiftly and they laughed aloud as Jenny approached.

Jade did her best to don a professional demeanour, but was feeling strangely bereft at the curtailing of their conversation and thinking how apt that last line was. Someone had indeed come along and burst their bubble of

. . . she didn't dare think what it actually was . . . and now she was going to be left with only its remnants.

Jenny slammed a sheet of A5 on her desk, white bob swishing as she twirled away from them almost as soon as she had arrived.

'Assignment for you two, tomorrow. I want Carl on the photos. Don't take too long.'

'Right.' Jade raised her own eyebrows at Carl, satisfied that her amusement was again shared. It was worse than being at school, being around Jenny Jackson, with her hasty instructions and tactless manner. Even Jade's teachers had been better communicators than that.

She scanned the piece of paper, attempting to decipher the writing. Eventually, admitting defeat, she passed it over to Carl.

'Oh, looks like the proposed property development on the west side of town. She wants you to interview someone relevant on the city council and me to take photos of what it's going to muck up.'

'Hmmm. Thrilling morning, then,' Jade joked, but secretly she knew there was some truth in it. Although it was wrong, and she felt the erroneousness deep in her gut, the thought of spending the morning with Carl Heaney, away from the office, was sending her into a spin.

'Could be.' He grinned then went on with barely a pause, leaving her slightly uncertain as to his meaning. 'We'll go in my four by four. The weather's supposed to be pants and we want you safe if we're out and about.'

Jade started, flustered by his comment, unsure how to respond.

We want you safe if we're out and about. The intimacy of his words swept up her body, heating her skin, making its way into every nook and cranny. Jade knew that she was confusing the sensation of being protected with desire but it all seemed to merge into one. Her own words failed her and she nodded, gathering stray paperclips pointlessly from under her monitor.

'Nice Santa gift, by the way,' he delivered as a parting shot, slipping from her desk and taking it back up the aisle.

She looked at the lingerie shrouded in tissue paper, imagining him seeing her in it, feeling the heat of her thoughts spread into an ache.

The flush on her face stopped her from turning to watch his retreat and she stared at the screen for two or three minutes, astounded by the knowledge that a trip in Carl Heaney's four by four had the potential to set her alight.

It was far from right, and she knew it, but she wallowed in the sensation unashamedly, until the return of Jenny Jackson with further brief instructions on the morning.

Shocked into action due to her unfinished workload, she forced her mind into professional focus and began the churn-out of the day's articles, sustained by syrupy coffee from the office machine.

* * *

Closing the door to her two up, two down on Eastland Road, Jade pressed speed-dial before she flopped down on the settee.

Rush hour traffic churned past at the top of the street and she listened to it, almost mesmerised, until the ring tone sounded in her ear. She imagined it ringing in her family home, and Dan's excitement, trying to race their mother to the phone, in his wheelchair.

'Mum?'

'Jade? Is that you?'

Jade smiled at the different, slightly cracked speech that came down the phone. Dan's voice was breaking, sure enough, and it was so tempting to make a joke of it, but she was never certain what she could get away with until she knew how his day had gone. Erring on the safe side, she rose above her couple of obvious jokes.

'Beat Mum to it, then? I reckon you're getting faster,' she encouraged, her heart secretly dropping at the reality. In truth, he was slowing down and Linda had been letting Dan beat her. Once upon a time, she used to complain that she never got the chance to answer it herself.

'I've decided,' Dan announced, sounding full of importance, 'I'm going to wheelchair-race in the next Olympics. I'm going to Rio. I'm going to start saving now for the plane ticket. Will you come with me?'

'Try and keep me away!' Jade lifted her voice a notch, trying hard not to let it crack for a different reason. She knew her brother hadn't a hope of racing even locally in four years' time. His long term prognosis wasn't fantastic — something he wasn't yet aware of — so Jade and their mother were determined to make the most of the years they did have.

Nevertheless, her heart lifted as she reconsidered Dan's words. Rio was something they could all aim for, to watch and cheer Team GB on. It was important to have goals, Mr Larson, the consultant had told them, and Dan had loved watching the triumphs of the athletes earlier in the year. He had been totally caught up in the highs and lows of the moment and been so motivated by the Paralympics that he had begged their mother to tape it all every day when he was at school.

'So, what have you been up to today?' she asked, waiting for the usual answer.

'Bo-o-oring. Maths, biology, RS and PE.'

'Ah . . . bet you can't wait to be out in the big wide world working,' Jade laughed. 'It's so much more fun,' she teased. 'Don't forget, Christmas Day we've a table at the Oak. The works. Turkey, Yorkshires, all the trimmings.'

'Yum. Is Brad going to be there?'

'Course he is. He can't wait to see you.'

Jade lowered her voice, ashamed of the slight untruth. It made her sad to see how Dan tried to substitute Brad for the big brother he never had, but

Brad hadn't managed yet to slip into the role. He tried — she knew he did, in his own way — but usually ended up treating Dan like someone lacking intelligence as he didn't know quite where to start.

'And I've got something very special for you,' she said, mysteriously, knowing it would appeal to Dan. 'But it doesn't matter how much you beg. You won't get it before the big day.'

'Awwwww. Jade! Come on, what is it? You can at least say what it is!'

'Dream on,' she laughed. 'Anyway, is Mum there? Can you give her a shout?'

'Mum!'

The word screeched through the phone and Jade held the phone away from her ear for a moment, smiling. It was good to hear Dan sounding so energetic. There were days when he was anything but.

'Hi babe. What's occurring?'

Jade spluttered with laughter at Linda's greeting, especially when her mum punctuated it with an exaggerated sigh.

'For goodness sake, Mum, you're not on TV. You're a forty-five-year-old doctor's receptionist who — '

'Don't I know it!' Linda complained. 'Bloomin' miserable so-and-so's complaining all day. All I see is people with something wrong with them. I should have got a job in a spa where folk float about all day, dipping in and out of steam baths and saunas without a care in the world.'

'Well, I'm not so sure about the last bit.' Jade grinned at her mother's naivety. 'Just because they're flitting in and out of the treatment rooms, doesn't mean they don't have a care in the world. Their cares and stresses are probably why they're there in the first place.'

'Whatever.'

Jade raised her eyebrows, smiling. Her mother's simplicity was probably what helped her get through the ordeal of bringing Dan up without a man to support her. Things were always black and white and she never looked too far ahead, tending to stay in the moment. It could be frustrating for those around her but, at times, Jade found it refreshing, wishing she could be more like her mother instead of worrying about the future long before it arrived.

'What's happening with you tonight, then, young lady?'

Linda was apparently bustling around the kitchen as she asked the question because Jade heard cupboard doors opening and closing.

'What can we have for dinner, Dan? There's nothing much here I fancy. What about a Chinese takeaway?'

'Mum! Feed him properly! He needs his five-a-day and, anyway, you haven't got money to keep chucking around on takeout food.' Jade tried hard to keep the exasperation from her voice. 'I know you need a break, Mum,' she added, softly. 'I'll come round tomorrow after work and cook something nice for you both.'

'Nice one, Jade. You're a good girl. I'm lucky to have you.' Linda's voice drifted in and out as she busied herself, losing concentration sporadically. 'Sixish tomorrow, then?'

'Hang on. You haven't talked to me yet! Dan sounds ok, today. Is everything OK with you, too?'

'You worry too much. We're fine. Anyway, you never said what you were up to tonight.'

'Just Brad's place. He's off overnight tomorrow so we're having a night in at his.'

Jade held her breath, waiting for her mother's inappropriateness to make its inevitable appearance.

'Well, if I were you I'd . . . ' Linda began, but Jade cut her mother short.

'Good job you're not, Mum. Take care and I'll see you both tomorrow after work. Give Dan a big kiss from me.'

'He'll love that,' Linda retorted, sarcastically. 'Don't do anything I wouldn't.'

Jade resisted the temptation to tell her about her Santa gift and pressed the red button with an ironic smile.

Looking around the lounge, she was glad she'd taken the opportunity to have a good tidy up the previous evening, with the newspaper pile cleared and the hoovering done. Dusting had been fleeting, but tackled nevertheless so, buoyed by the memory of Dan's cheerful voice and her day in the office, she entered the bedroom, threw on some jeans and a white mohair jumper, then emptied the lunchbox out of her work bag.

When her pack-up was done for the next day, she put it back into her bag ready for the morning, grabbed her keys, said goodbye to her rubber plant and closed the door on the home she was so proud of.

She'd had a mortgage for eighteen months now and, scary as it had been at the beginning, she was glad she had made the move from the family home. Living with Linda had had its frustrations and they got on so much better now that each had their own space.

Jade headed in her car onto the A30, making her way to the quaint market town of Sherborne where Brad had his flat. It was ten minutes, tops, and she made it in eight.

After squeezing her Corsa into a parking slot a short walk away from Brad's, she lowered her head against the wind and battled her way up Cheap Street.

3

Jade stood in the lounge doorway as Brad pulled on his running shorts, thinking George Foreman had almost got it right. Lean, mean, running machine certainly described her boyfriend to a tee.

She tossed her bag onto the settee, watching as the hard lines of his bronzed torso disappeared under his T-shirt, and smiling at the logo. *Just do it* also summed him up nicely and, as he bounced on the spot, she began to feel itchy for running herself. She hadn't relaxed since that morning; something inside her was on fire, like the huge black Olympic cauldron Dan had thought was 'awesome', and she was at a loss to know what would put it out.

'Off out, then?' she asked, slightly sarcastically, having only just arrived.

'Yeah, just for a run. A quick one. Won't be long. Make yourself at home, Jade.' Brad leant across to peck her on the cheek. 'There's a fresh smoothie in the fridge.'

'When isn't there?' Jade laughed, but she didn't really fancy it. She didn't fancy anything very much and could barely keep herself still. 'Hold on, Brad. I might come with you. I must have something upstairs in the drawer.'

Leaping up the stairs two at a time, she flew to the bedroom and flung open the drawer Brad had vacated for her overnight stays. There were a couple of tops that could pass as a T-shirt and thin leggings that hadn't been worn for a few months. She knew there were trainers by the front door, along with a couple of pairs of her sandals, so she tossed her jumper and jeans onto the bed and donned the more sporty gear.

Downstairs inside three minutes, she pulled on her trainers without socks.

'Better than nothing,' she said.

'You haven't come running with me

for ages.' Brad's voice rose and fell as he grabbed the key, still bouncing up and down on the spot. 'Nice though. It'll do you the world of good.'

'I'm sure it will,' she retorted, raising her eyebrows as she eased her way past him. 'Come on you lazy lump. Get your ass out of this door.'

The communal hall was empty and Brad closed the door to his flat, pulled a lanyard over his head and tucked the key inside his T-shirt.

Outside, the air was so fresh, it sucked the air from Jade's lungs as she began running, reminding her of Carl's closeness only that morning.

It seemed a lifetime ago in some ways, but in others she could still feel the warmth of his breath on the back of her neck. The deep brown of his eyes seemed to taunt her, coming into view as she ran, and she pounded the pavement with gusto, sometimes just ahead of Brad, sometimes behind, which made a change from the usual view of his rear.

Having not run for some months, she was astonished at how easily it was coming. The clean, clear air of the evening seemed to cleanse every cell of her body, making her fly.

'What's got into you tonight?' Brad laughed as they tumbled into his flat half an hour later, sweat glistening on both their bodies. 'You were like a bat out of hell.'

He threw the key onto the kitchen counter, pulled open the fridge and poured them both a tall glass of blueberry juice freshly made earlier.

'Nothing . . . yet,' she responded, risking some cheekiness, downing her glassful in one with a wink. With the adrenalin from the run still whizzing around her body, she felt a bit naughty and extraordinarily alive. She couldn't remember the last time she'd felt like this and she liked the sensation. Each of her senses was sharpened; outside on their run she'd felt the sharp breeze on her fingertips, tasted the thick winter air, felt she could touch every one of the stars in the crisp sky above. Something inside her was making her want to sing and she revelled in the feeling, mentally avoiding the truth of its cause.

Brad swished his empty glass under the tap and left it to drain by the sink. His agile body moved swiftly around the kitchen, gathering utensils and crockery as he went, and she watched him with a thirst that the juice hadn't quenched.

'Hungry?' he said. 'I've made organic chicken stroganoff. I know you like beef but white meat is so much healthier. You'll love it. You'll see.'

'Sounds good.' Jade was unsurprised at the offering as Brad made most of his meals from scratch. It was one of the things that had first amazed her when he'd started bringing her home, — the time he took over creating his meals.

She soon understood that it was his obsession with perfection that drove him to control everything he put in his body, and he could afford the best as

40

Mummy and Daddy tossed him the odd cheque every now and again.

Jade quashed her envy as soon as it reared its hideous head, thinking of her own little family and their humble home. It may all be rather meagre in comparison, but it was loving, supportive and real.

In contrast, Brad's home was extraordinarily superficial, all business, targets and victories, burgeoning with success but little sincerity and even less warmth.

Perhaps that was another reason why he found it so hard to relax at Linda and Dan's. It was all so different and personal from what he was used to at home.

Jade switched on the TV as Brad heated the stroganoff. She caught up with the local news, drifting in and out of concentration, her mind wandering. Tonight, everything around her heightened her senses, from a soap opera character's blouse with one too many buttons undone, to the swing of Brad's hair, bleached blonder than ever from

41

hours lying on scorching white sand. It hung over one side of his face as he plopped down beside her, his hand still hot from their run when he passed her a plate, and her fingers brushed it back from his eye, their sensitive tips touching his cheek. His skin was smooth and she guessed he had shaved off his five o'clock shadow after work.

'Thought it'd be nicest with rice,' he said, as she took it and tucked in.

The sauce was creamy and brimming with taste, but Jade knew Brad would somehow have made it low calorie. It was probably more due to his culinary skills than anything else that she was as slim as she was.

There was no doubt about it, Brad was a great cook, but within four bites her appetite had diminished. Within eight, her stomach felt full, her hunger gone, but she slowly ploughed on, knowing how upset Brad would be if she left it. She stopped before she felt bloated as that was a feeling she couldn't abide.

'That was amazing, but it's about all

I can manage,' she said, pushing the remnants into the smallest pile she could manage, hoping it would appear less than it was.

She took it to the sink and had returned before Brad had finished. It was a habit of his, to eat slowly, in order that he would eat less, and it was a continual bugbear to him that he couldn't eat upright at a table. There was no way of fitting a table into his flat, try as he might.

Jade flopped back down beside him, still distracted and aroused. Flashes of Carl's brown eyes drilling into her whisked through her heightened consciousness and she shifted closer to Brad in an attempt to force them away. The sweat had dried on his arms now but the dark patch of its remnants remained down the centre of his T-shirt.

She placed her hand at the top of his shorts then slipped it under the cotton of his T-shirt, touching the tautness of his abdomen, and he drew in a breath then let it out slowly as her palm

43

travelled upwards, over the smoothness of his stomach, to his chest, where she let it stay still for a few moments, feeling his breathing quicken beneath her hand.

'Steady on, Jade,' Brad admonished, the crack in his voice failing to convince. 'I spent time making this,' he nodded down to the plate of food in his hand.

'It'll keep.' Jade shifted closer, her lips finding his neck, but Brad edged away, shrugging her off.

'Jade! I haven't finished yet. What on earth has got into you tonight?'

The question hit Jade right in the sternum, reminding her of how long it had been since she and Brad had been together. She had been waiting for him to initiate contact for weeks, thinking that he had been working too hard at the office, but tonight she'd had more than enough of waiting. She racked her brains, thinking of how she could get Brad going again.

'How about I get my new undies?

They're still in my bag,' she teased.

'Oh, Jade, I'm up early tomorrow.' Brad placed his now empty plate and cutlery on the floor beside the settee.

For a second, the frustration of Brad leaving the following day to cover a tournament overnight in Yorkshire stopped Jade in her tracks, then her mind went back to the lingerie.

Getting Brad worked up might be conducive for a confession.

'They were from you, weren't they?' she stated more than asked. 'Brilliant choice . . . I love the pretty pink ties either side of the panties.'

'Hmmmm.' Brad kissed the top of her head. 'Good try, sorceress, but it's not working. It's Secret Santa, remember. I'm not a squealer.'

Jade's breath heated his skin as she made another assault on his neck with her lips.

'Like you didn't squeal about the Valentine's card, the rose in April and the soppy CD . . . '

Her mind recalled times in the year

when she'd discovered a present left on her desk in the office. It had always been when Brad was off on overnight assignments, so he must have had someone in on it. It wouldn't have been Sara Maxwell, that was for sure. He was such a romantic, Jade sensed it deep down, but he never let things like that show.

'I don't sign Valentine's cards,' he teased as he edged away. 'Else what's the point?'

Not one to be daunted, Jade rose and went to find her bag.

'Where are you going?' Brad asked, heading for the sink with his plate that he'd retrieved from the floor.

'I just told you,' Jade said. 'We can see what my Secret Santa present looks like on.'

Still receiving no encouragement, Jade suddenly felt like a floozy touting for business, convinced that it shouldn't be this hard to turn a man on, especially when he was her boyfriend, for good-ness' sake! A stain of embarrassment coloured her cheeks, but Brad's next words made it much worse.

'Not tonight, Jade,' he said, switching the TV channel to sport. 'We're all sweaty from our run. Why don't we save them for when I get back after the trip? It'll be something to look forward to.'

He put out an arm for her to join him and Jade stared at him for a moment, the fire within her well and truly doused.

4

The rain slashed onto the windscreen, obscuring Jade's view, and she flipped the wiper switch into fast mode with one hand and the indicator with the other. Slowly, she eased to the side of the road, mindful of the pedestrians walking close to the puddles at the kerb, then pulled on the handbrake.

Brad turned to her, leaning across the gearstick to peck her on the cheek.

'Thanks for dropping me off.' His hand was warm, unlike her own, as he squeezed her hand. 'I'll miss you. We'll try that underwear out when I get back.'

As if it was a new hoover that needed testing, Jade thought.

She smiled half-heartedly, feeling the ache of disappointment once again, alongside the other ache that she preferred not to define. It hadn't really ever left her since the previous morning and she'd had little sleep in the deep, dark hours of the night, trying hard not to disturb Brad.

Having promised that she would sleep over, she had soon regretted it, tossing and turning all night in the darkness. Her own place would have been better for filling the hours that had felt more like weeks without the promise of sleep.

Now, at the wheel, she was percolating with coffee to keep her awake. Brad had heartily disapproved, having caught her using her own caffeinated brand.

'Have a good trip. Hope the netball team win.'

She kissed him back then watched as he threw open the door, narrowly missing a passer-by. After slamming it shut again, he opened the rear door and tugged out his bag.

'They're pretty good,' he replied, 'but we'll see. Have a good day at work.'

Jade flushed, convinced that Brad could see through her, certain he could tell she was itching to get into the office and had been feeling that way most of the night.

Yet, it was ridiculous and she knew it. Carl Heaney was just a regular guy in the office who was pretty damn good with a camera. He had nothing to do with Jade Cooke other than being a colleague who sometimes came for a chat.

She had no right to think anything else. She was with Brad, and it wasn't his fault that girls like Sara Maxwell flocked after him. Who could blame them, after all? But his attractiveness hadn't affected Jade that way when she had been getting to know him. Brad's 'A list' looks, far from bowling her over, had made her tougher to convince when he'd finally asked her out.

Jade knew she would miss Brad and didn't want him to go. He had slammed the rear door shut and turned into the rain, making for the alleyway that would take him to the car park and station entrance.

Now, at the last moment, he turned, gave her a wave and blew a surreptitious kiss. Jade blew one back, smiling indulgently at his wayward blond hair, now hanging in dark, damp threads.

At once, the car seemed emptier than ever. She felt strange, in a way that she couldn't recall feeling before. Everything seemed so much more real as she wove her way through the traffic to the office, yet at the same time she felt oddly distant. The world was alive, and she was alive in it, but the two didn't connect. She was a viewer, a reader, watching a tale unfold, although she suspected that she was the character, seeing her own story revealed as it played out.

By the time she pulled up in the multi-storey car park, she admonished herself for such airy-fairy nonsense. Lack of sleep was quite obviously playing tricks on her mind.

Forcing herself not to glance across at Carl Heaney's desk when she entered the office, she felt childishly smug with her achievement when she made it to her own desk without looking; but she needn't have bothered.

Carl was there, in all his six foot glory, running his hand through the soft spikes in his hair.

At least they looked soft, Jade thought to herself, trying not to be obvious, but it was impossible to know without touching — and oh, how she'd love to — in the same way that his muscles looked hard and uncompromising, yet they may be deceptive. After all, how would she know if she never did touch?

'Appointment's been brought forward from eleven to ten.'

'You were right. You said the weather would be bad.' Jade dropped her bag onto the floor next to her chair.

'Mornin'.' Carl smiled, his white teeth doubling as an advert.

'Morning.' Jade felt the smile break through her tiredness and wake up her eyes. 'Do we have an angle?'

'You're the writer,' Carl said, lifting

his digital camera. 'I'm just the bod who takes pics.'

'Right. Just the bod.' Jade feared her lop-sided grin might give away her thoughts on what sort of bod Carl actually had. So, only half an hour to kill before they had to get going. That really wasn't so bad. 'We're seeing a protester then a councillor. I sorted it before leaving last night.'

'That's what I love about you, Jade Cooke. You take the bull by the horns.'

'And I'm so glad you're doing the pics and not the writing. We wouldn't want a piece full of clichés now, would we?' she laughed. 'Anyway, why are you carrying that around?' She nodded to the camera now sat on her desk beneath the photograph of Dan.

'Not an idea. To be honest, it's more impressive when the zoom is attached. The ladies like that, I'm told. Some sort of symbolism . . . ' He gave her a wicked look.

'I wouldn't know,' Jade insisted, feigning innocence but drawn in by the sparkle in his dark eyes. 'I know nothing about magnification and electronic image sensors, let alone over exposure or photo manipulation.'

Carl laughed, the sound making her own laugh bubble up in her throat.

'You're a shark,' he said. 'A deceiver. Is there anything you don't know?'

How to get you out of my head when I'm not with you, Jade thought, inhaling Carl's morning coffee not a metre from her nose. 'You could have got me one,' she diverted, nodding towards his cup. 'I've only had two so far.'

'No sooner said, m'lady,' he said, and was gone.

Jade looked around the office as she unpacked her bag, colour touching her cheeks as she realised her lingerie gift was still in it. The tissue rustled as she placed her lunchbox under her desk.

'Smells good,' she said gratefully, cupping the styrofoam between her hands when Carl returned. 'It's nasty out there. I could do with a warm up before facing that again.'

'Well, I've stuff to get on with before I take you out in my carriage. Don't forget your glass slippers.'

He collected his camera and Jade watched the movement of the muscles in his back under his shirt as he strode down the aisle, making her wonder how they might feel.

From the corner of her eye, she could sense someone's eyes upon her and turned away promptly, trying to seem uninterested in anything other than loading her screen, but Sara Maxwell strode past before she'd barely pressed the button.

'Have a nice morning out,' Sara drawled, her voice more efficiently loaded than the PC Jade was trying to start.

Jade threw back her best smile, sensing it would be best to say nothing other than, 'Hardly the best day for an assignment,' alluding to the weather. It turned out not to be neutral enough.

'Depends who you're with, I s'pose,'

Sara quipped, shooting a meaningful glance towards Carl a few cubicles down and Jade was left to wonder at how blatant her contemplations on Carl had been. She felt reassured that they weren't as obvious as Sara's for Brad, but nevertheless she was determined to get on and concentrate until nine thirty arrived.

★ ★ ★

At nine forty, out on the road, the four by four ploughed through the town and the flooded road by the hospital roundabout.

'About time they unblocked that drain,' Carl said conversationally, and Jade nodded her response.

She had said little since leaving the office. Sara's comment had knocked her for six and she was resolute in her decision to start acting her age around Carl instead of being doe-eyed and pathetic. Yes, he stopped her pulse in its tracks whenever she laid eyes on him and, yes, her lungs emptied of air when his brown eyes caught her own, but she was Brad's girlfriend and, to make it worse, the guy was on his way up to Yorkshire. It was a pretty poor show if he couldn't trust her the moment he stepped out of the door.

She would just have to control herself — it was only a physical response, after all, which happened to millions all over the world every moment — so she focused on the road ahead, not daring to glance across at the man not three feet away from her.

His musky aftershave permeated the air in the car, but she ignored it, trying to recall the smell of Brad's deodorant after his shower the previous night. She couldn't quite manage it but, unperturbed, she attempted to replay the evening.

It only made matters worse.

Her notes failed to keep her attention so, when they were almost at the planned development site, she stuffed them into her work bag and looked through the lines of trickling droplets at the granite clouds beyond.

'Can't see me getting any good shots in this,' Carl commented, peering around her at the fields beyond, then she felt rather than saw him focus his gaze on her. 'I was going to get a few in now, but I think I'll wait until after you've worked your magic in the interviews. The forecast says it might clear a bit.' He cleared his throat, sounding a little uncomfortable, and Jade sensed that he'd noticed the change in her demeanour. 'Is that ok with you?' he asked, changing gear.

'Of course.' Jade shot him a thin smile, then turned back to the window.

Twenty seconds later they pulled into a lay-by and, low and behold, six protesters stood in the rain with their boards.

'Dedication. Good for them.' Jade pulled up her hood and gripped the door handle. 'I'll interview the bloke in his car. Shouldn't be long.'

'Right you are. I'll be here, waiting.'

Despite herself, Jade caught his gaze as she closed the car door, startled by the intimate tone of his voice. She lowered her own gaze then fought her way through the sheeting rain to the car that sat further along the road in an opposite lay-by. The elements failed to make any impact on her cheeks, rosy from the car heater and Carl's words as she'd left his four by four. Doing her best to appear professional, she approached one of the two men of the group, aware that she had a fifty-fifty chance of having found her interviewee.

'Martin Hammond?'

'That's me. You must be Jade.'

Jade nodded towards the car parked nearby. 'I am. Is that yours?'

'Fancy somewhere drier? You office types,' he teased. 'Come on then.'

He led the way, crossing the road to the opposite kerb and Jade saw the unevenness of his gait. He was fifty to sixty, black hair peppered liberally with grey, a stone or two overweight. Arthritis, she wondered, seeing how he winced on levering himself into the car.

Once inside with him, Jade drew the dictaphone from her pocket and pulled off her hood.

'You OK with this?' she asked, holding up the piece of hardware and Martin nodded. Through the rain-splattered windscreen, Jade saw Carl's camera through the car window, pointed towards them. Perhaps she should have borrowed it and taken one of Martin herself.

'Fine by me,' he assured her, helpfully. 'Fire away.'

5

Inevitably, the interview with the councillor's pro-development stance was the harder of the two. Jade always found interviewees on the defensive were pricklier than those on the attack but she'd got some good quotes from both and was keen to get them typed up.

By the time Carl had taken his photos, her stomach was making known its discontent with the time that had passed since Brad's preparation of muesli that morning. Her embarrassment now was severe when the rumblings caught Carl's attention, breaking his rather sombre demeanour since her return to the car.

'Sounds like someone needs a refuel,' he joked, his face straight as he shot her a sideways look. 'I know how to treat a girl. Fancy swinging by Maccy D's for a Happy Meal?'

Jade couldn't help but laugh at the

mock seriousness of his tone.

'I'd rather have a whopper,' she responded, with an equally earnest face.

'I'm sure I can oblige,' he replied, sending such a curiously thrilling glance in her direction that she felt the back of her neck grow warm.

'Come on, then,' she giggled, girlishly. 'What are we waiting for? I don't get an offer like that every day!'

As his face dissolved into a grin Jade knew her resolve had cracked once again. There was just something about him that drew triviality out of her. Somehow she could barely control what came out of her mouth.

They had beaten the lunchtime diners. Turning in at the lights on the dual carriageway, there were a few slots where they could park. Carl suggested they go inside.

'Not keen on my carriage stinking of chips. Besides, what would your fairy godmother say if you went home smelling of burgers?'

Carl locked the car with the remote

as they entered the fast-food chain and Jade felt in her trousers pocket for some change.

'If she was anything like my mother, she wouldn't notice if I went home dressed as one,' Jade replied, scanning the board whilst trying not to show she could feel how close Carl was standing. She placed some money on the counter.

'Ah, no. My treat.' Carl scooped up the coins and returned them to her hand. The coins fell into her palm and his fingers touched hers for what must have been less than a second but, for Jade, time stood still. She was transfixed by the voltage that shot through her like a bullet from a magnum and, despite the rigidity of her body, her mind was awhirl with one thought that started to circulate.

Now I know what it feels like; the power of his touch.

But she knew it would have been better if the discovery had never been made. Even worse, she saw it in his eyes too.

They were different, softer, more personal, as if a secret had just been exposed.

Neither moved for an eternity as the revelation silently fermented between them but, finally, Jade was aware of the girl serving at the counter preparing their tray, asking what they might like, and she reluctantly moved from the bubble that had built itself around them.

Her breath fluttered in her chest, making her feel light-headed as she made her order. She must pretend, she told herself firmly, making a show of choosing a straw, deciding which colour. She must pretend that she had felt nothing. Nothing had been said so it wasn't too late.

By the time they had settled at a table and taken their food off the tray, Jade sensed a sort of equilibrium had been restored. She relaxed into it, tucking into her food but finding herself not as hungry as her stomach had insisted.

Carl polished off his burger but seemed to renege on his fries, rubbing his ear in a nervous manner as he played with his sachet of salt.

Jade had tried not to fix her attention on the impressive cut of his jaw as he'd chewed, but had failed miserably and was now unbearably mesmerised by the gentle slope of his nose. Her finger itched to trace its contour, right down to the cute little dip just above his inviting lips and, as she furtively watched, the tip of his tongue slipped out and dampened them, licking away the stray salt.

'Jade? Are you ok?' he asked, taking her by surprise.

She threw back a mouthful of orange juice, her concentration directed at the cleaner sweeping near their table. The bloke was a less than convincing diversion but how could she answer the question and not open a can full of worms?

At last, she decided upon an alternative subject that took up the other part of her mind space.

'I'm fine, Carl,' she said, playing origami games with her napkin with the expertise of a four year old. 'It's just

Dan, I suppose. I worry about him. And about Mum too, if I'm honest. Even after Dan's deterioration this past year, she still seems to be in denial and convinced that all will be well.'

'Hmmm.' Carl played with his own napkin, mirroring Jade's amateur folding techniques. 'It's a worry, to be sure. If you want to know what I think, I think they're lucky to have you.'

Jade smiled her gratitude, frustrated to find he would no longer look at her. His brow furrowed and she could almost touch the anticipation in the air at his next words, but they didn't reach her. Instead, he remained silent and she felt compelled to go on.

Near the counter, the noise level heightened as a group of schoolkids piled through the door. There were no schools very close and she wondered how they would have got there in their lunch hour, but the thought was fleeting as her mind returned to her brother, Slade playing their eternal Christmas song from the speakers above their heads.

'I know that he doesn't need to be spoilt, just because of his illness, but I can't help but want to make what he can still do enjoyable. I've bought him an iPad3 for Christmas, but I wanted to get him something special as well. Something more personal, but I can't think what. Last year, I bought him an engraved silver pen and for his birthday I gave him a day out in a racing car.'

Carl's hands were slightly distracting, no longer playing with the napkin, his fingers interlacing and opening back up. Now that she knew what it felt like to touch them, the reality of it swept through her and she longed to lace her own fingers between them.

'Well,' she continued, swiftly, 'a professional guy drove him round the circuit a couple of times, that is, but he loved it. He adores Formula 1 but I don't think Lewis Hamilton will be free on Christmas Day to pop over.'

She smiled, aware it was unconvincing, and accompanying it with a sigh.

'Tricky,' Carl said, simply, and left it at that. Disconcerted, Jade suddenly felt the need to fill the gap.

'I shouldn't complain. I know that. I'm lucky I've got enough money to buy him things like an iPad, but . . . oh, I don't know. I just wanted something . . . '

'How about a portrait of yourself?' Carl sat back in his seat, folded his arms and appeared to contemplate her until the heat of a blush began on her cheeks.

She felt he was sizing her up professionally, and automatically felt herself wanting. Who else had he photographed, she wondered, throughout his career?

'He'd like that, wouldn't he?' Carl went on, suddenly enthused by the idea. 'A picture of you? I could get it done in time. You'd need to get it framed though, but there's always the net if you pay for fast delivery.'

'Really?' Jade heard the rise in her tone, his enthusiasm contagious. It wasn't anything she'd ever considered, but Dan would like it, she was sure. 'How much . . . ?'

'I hope you're not asking what I think you are!' Carl interrupted, feigning annoyance. 'For goodness' sake, Jade. If you've to think of it some way, think of it as my Christmas present to you.'

No matter the manner of how it came out, the sound of her name on Carl's lips brought goosebumps to her skin and she rubbed her arms over her sweater, thinking bizarrely he might somehow see. He had said her name before, of course, but each time the effect on her became magnified. How could one syllable actually grow in stature and strength?

'Well, if you're sure,' she said, weakly. 'That'd be fabulous, Carl. What a kind thought.'

In that moment, she realised that she really did mean it. It was a kind thought, just as she'd seen over time that he was a kind, thoughtful guy. The recognition warmed her still further and she met his gaze bravely, the invisible, heavenly thread between them seeming to link her psyche to his.

'Pop round after work.' Carl finally spoke. 'I'll give you my address when we get back to the office. If Dan likes it, we could always take one of you both together later on.'

Carl glanced at his watch and she saw his lips part with exasperation as a small sigh escaped.

'I'm thinking we'd better get on or Jenny'll be on our backs.' He scraped back his chair, leaving Jade with a vision of Carl's back as she pushed back her own chair, liking the image and the sensations that it produced. If the electricity from the touch of their hands was anything to go by, her palms running over his back would surely frazzle her to the core.

Frantically, she went through her timings after work, wondering what time she could make it over for the portrait.

'I've promised to cook for Mum and Dan this evening, and then I'll need to get changed and throw on a bit of make-up before I come over to you.'

She thought on her feet, careful not to brush against him as she held open the door, bracing herself against the cold wind as they emerged into the car park. 'Is about eight thirty ok?'

'Fine by me.'

Oh my Lord, the audacious side of her muttered, as she slid onto Carl's warm leather seat. *Dangerous territory,* the erudite side of her mumbled in haughty response.

The journey back elapsed in what seemed like a moment and the reluctance was palpable as they re-entered the office, re-acquiring their work personas as they walked through the door.

It's just a photograph, Jade told herself as Carl left her side to load images from the morning onto his computer, but her subconscious remained unconvinced as her brain produced its own images throughout the rest of the day.

6

'Hi, how's today been?' Brad's voice rang out, loud and strong, on the pavement outside Jade's family home and she swiftly turned the volume down on the side of her mobile. The front door opened and she slipped inside, indicating to Dan that she was talking, then bent down to give him a kiss. She was rewarded by an eager hug that said he had missed her since the weekend.

'Not too bad,' she replied into the phone. 'Did the interviews with the councillor and protester. It tipped it with rain. The rest of the afternoon I wrote up the article, then caught up on one or two others that need to be finished this week. How about you?'

She silently acknowledged her omission, but he had, after all, asked what she had already done, not what she was yet to be doing. She would tell him, of course, that she would be going to Carl's later to shoot a portrait, but she'd listen to his day first.

'Where's Mum?' she whispered to Dan, holding her hand over the mouthpiece.

'In the bath,' he replied raising an eyebrow. 'Can't you smell it? It smells like — '

'Don't even say it!' Jade laughed, turning her attention back to the phone.

' . . . with the netball team,' Brad was saying, and she could hear the buzz of conversation in the background. 'They invited me to join them tonight for a basket meal in the pub and it seemed churlish to refuse.'

Jade smiled, despite herself, unable to imagine Brad on a netball team night out.

'So . . . did they win?'

'I believe they did.'

Jade raised her eyebrows at his uncertainty.

'I'm sure you had other important

things to be thinking about,' she quipped, imagining the short skirts and frilly knickers. *Did they still wear stuff like that nowadays,* she wondered, deciding she would ask him when he got back.

What's with the green monster? Jade asked herself. Normally, thoughts like that wouldn't enter her head. Just because her own mind was wandering in all sorts of unhelpful directions, didn't mean that Brad Wilson's mind was as well.

Determined that she would stick to a sensible conversation with Dan in the room, albeit he was sufficiently occupied by his Xbox, she remained silent. He appeared to be thrashing Arsenal 5-1 on Fifa 2013.

'Important things, like my girlfriend,' Brad quipped back, taking her by surprise. 'I miss you.'

Jade closed her eyes, imagining herself back in his arms.

'I miss you, too. Are you still back tomorrow?' Mentally, her fingers were crossed. It would help, him being back here in Yeovil, reining her in, saving her from herself.

'I dunno, yet.'

His sigh was audible and she thought of him surrounded by young, fit women, yet still wanting to be back here with her and her heart stuttered for a moment, jolted by the thought of his linear mind.

'I was messing. I know that they won all their games today 'cos I lived every single point. Who'd have thought it? Women's netball!'

Jade knew him too well and smiled at his fake male chauvinism.

'If they win tomorrow, they'll be in the final and I'll have to stay on for that. I'll email my report back today for the Observer's internet site.'

'Oh.' Jade nodded to Dan who had finished his game and wanted her to join in. She held up a hand to stall him for a moment. 'Well, I can't really will them to lose, can I?'

She laughed rather feebly, fearing the

vulnerability of herself back home as much as the attention Brad would receive in the meantime.

'I'll have to go now as I'm cooking for Mum and Dan. Dan's heading for the kitchen so I expect I'm in for a battle, stopping him picking at junk before dinner.'

It was something she'd been worried about — her brother's lack of exercise now that he was mostly confined to his wheelchair — and she'd liaised with his consultant herself to explore how they could help prevent him gaining weight.

The removal of junk food from the kitchen was top of the list, but Linda was yet to bring the idea into practice and Jade had to bite her tongue consistently whenever she came around.

'Ok, babe, well I can hear that chicken clucking around in its basket. It's on its way out. Think of me later, when you're snuggled up in that girly pink bed of yours.'

'I'll ring you,' she promised, feeling bad about cutting the conversation so short, but she had a lot to fit in this evening. By the time she had cooked, cleared and washed up, she'd have to dash back to hers, then on to Carl's place. Having realised that she hadn't mentioned what she was doing later, her plans were on the tip of her tongue, causing her pulse to accelerate, when a shriek almost pierced her eardrum.

'What was that?' she gasped in surprise.

'One of the netball lot getting a bit out of hand. I think they're loosening up a bit.' Brad laughed. 'The food's here. Better go. Catch you later.'

Jade's smile was shortlived. She hadn't told him about seeing Carl later that evening. At least Brad had had the decency to tell Jade where he was, but she'd kept her plans to herself.

Doing her best to push it out of her mind, she shoved her phone into her bag and went into the kitchen where, lo and behold, Dan was ferreting in the fridge where their mother kept all the chocolate and goodies.

'Dan Cooke!' Jade rebuked her brother harshly, aware she sounded cruel but was intending to be kind. 'Out of that fridge, young man,' she continued, more softly. 'It's vegetable curry for dinner — your favourite — so you won't have to wait long.'

Dan swung his wheelchair in her direction and she nodded before he'd even spoken.

'Yes, we've got fizzy apple juice. It's a treat, so don't expect it every time. You can get it out of my bag.'

Dan navigated around the table, drew out the bottle with a happy grin and took it to the fridge.

Jade sighed: potential disaster averted.

'You know the drill too well,' Jade smiled. 'I must be doing this far too often.'

'You can't have too many treats. What can I do? I'm bored, but I'm not doing my homework yet,' he added, apparently anticipating her reply.

'Ok. You can start peeling the veg, as long as you promise to do your homework when I leave at about seven thirty. I don't want Mum having to nag.'

'Seven thirty?' Dan's face fell almost as far as Jade's heart when she saw his expression. 'Can't you stay later?'

She crossed the room to the vegetable rack.

'Not tonight, love. I've an important appointment, but we'll make up for it on Christmas Day. Here you go . . . ' She tossed him a couple of carrots then slid the peeler over the table. 'Don't forget the chopping board,' she reminded him then set about preparing the rice and making the sauce.

They chatted as they worked, Jade keen to find out, discretely, how Dan was doing at school.

The curry was bubbling in the pan by the time their mother made an appearance, clad in a towel, smelling of sweet peas and with bright orange hair.

Jade stopped in mid flow, chopping board half in and half out of the water, mortified at the orange streaks trickling down Linda's neck. She looked like something out of a cheap horror movie and, unable yet to gauge her mother's own reaction, Jade wasn't sure whether or not she could fall about laughing without being murdered herself.

'I'm not quite sure that it's gone right,' Linda announced, wiping some of the streaks away with a tea towel that had hung behind the kitchen door. 'It says 'chestnut' on the box.'

Jade's jaw muscles ached from trying not to laugh but eventually a snort flagged up the start of it and she was a goner.

Dan joined her in moments and almost fell out of his chair.

'I expect it's confused by all the other colours beneath it,' Jade finally gasped, shooting a look at the curry. It could take care of itself for a while. 'Don't touch the pan, Dan,' she instructed. 'I'll sort Mum out while it's cooking. You see if Arsenal can get their revenge.'

By the time she had scrubbed the stains off Linda's skin and styled her hair to make her look less like a pump-kin, the rice needed cooking then Dan needed her undivided attention until it was time to serve up.

Arsenal, under her footballing non-expertise, had met their total demise and she retreated to the kitchen, thankful for talents elsewhere.

What was it with blokes and their games? she wondered, straining the rice and fetching the juice from the fridge.

Brad spent hours on his PS3, playing level after level, trading in game after game. It had to be something in their make-up that made them so skilled at working a handset in order to wipe out half the world, but she couldn't help wishing Brad could be a bit more dynamic in real life.

★　★　★

Seven thirty arrived before she knew it and Jade realised she had worn a small ragged hole in Carl's address in her back pocket with her continual fiddling.

She'd lost count of how many times she'd checked it was there, even though she now knew the address by heart.

When she'd said her goodbyes and left Dan with the promise of Christmas Day looming, the wind had died down to a whisper and the A30 was quiet as she made her way back to Yeovil and Eastland Road.

Jade's own little home looked sad and empty now that the shortest dark days had arrived. Quickly, she drew all the curtains and switched on a lamp in the lounge. She would leave it on now, for security, preferring to make it look as though someone was in.

A glance at the clock sent her scuttling upstairs with her work bag and a pair of lilac heels she wanted to see on in the mirror.

Her Santa lingerie taunted her inside the tissue and she drew it out and placed it on the bed.

She should wait for Brad to come back, especially as he had bought it, but she wanted to see what it looked like

— just for a moment — so she took off her work clothes, then her comfy, functional bra and knickers, dropping them lazily onto the floor.

The new bra went on first and it fitted to perfection, cupping her beautifully with an enticing swell of cleavage above. The panties were a bit of a fiddle as she messed about with the ties but, once they were on, she couldn't resist doing a twirl in front of the mirror. Her gentle curves more than did the underwear justice and she ran her hands over her contours, delighted with the result.

It felt good to dress up for a change and made her feel strangely corporeal, as though her body had forgotten how much it was really alive.

Then it was time to take them back off. Reluctantly placing them back in the tissue paper, Jade had to admit that wearing them to Carl Heaney's place for her portrait didn't feel right and she always remembered her old nan's advice when she was younger . . . don't put in the window what's not for sale.

She replaced them with a dainty white bra and white cotton panties, then a white camisole over the top. Having never been to Carl's place, she had no idea whether he used, or even possessed, central heating and didn't relish the thought of freezing all evening. Another layer never hurts, her nan had always said too.

She flicked through her wardrobe, searching for an outfit that matched the occasion, getting jumpier by the minute as she became aware of the time.

A pale yellow blouse jumped out at her that she felt set off her dark auburn hair, along with a thin black cardigan that hung down to her thighs. Once they were on, it had to be black skinny jeans and she held up the pale lilac shoes, shaking her head.

'Sorry guys,' Jade murmured, tossing them onto the bed. 'Can't say you'd suit.'

She brushed through her hair, removing the pins then reapplying them until her hair was as precise and painstakingly ordered as it was at the start of each day. A hundred per cent shine spray completed the look, but the shoes on the bed still looked somehow sad and discarded. In a fit of remorse, she shoved them onto her feet.

'Whoa!' she smiled, amazed at how natty they looked.

Pulling her new Santa gift make-up from her bag, she sat down in front of the dresser, turning her head this way and that, deciding upon the colour. It has to be brown, she thought, first applying a liner, then the powder to her eyelids. An infinite-length mascara framed her green eyes to perfection, then it was just the lip liner, lipstick and gloss.

A glance at the bedside clock sent her scuttling down the stairs to her coat and out to the car, then promptly back in again to retrieve Carl's address.

'Idiot!' she admonished herself, as she re-entered the bedroom. Her work clothes still lay on the floor where she'd dropped them and she retrieved the piece of paper from the jeans pocket and hung all her clothes up quickly in a fit of conscience. She never ironed unless she had to, so she may as well reduce the necessity where she could.

Scrumpled up paper in hand, she was back at the car within minutes and she slid into the seat, unasked-for scruples thrusting blood through her veins at the speed of a cougar.

Somehow this felt dangerous, but she started the engine regardless, heading the car west for Montacute, ignoring the quietly insistent self-reproach.

It was just a photo for her beautiful brother for Christmas, she reasoned. There was nothing to be scared of. Carl was no-one. Carl Heaney was just a colleague from work.

7

'Come on in.' Carl held open the door to his flat and stepped aside. Jade had parked in the drive and walked round the side, as per his instructions.

He owned part of an old Victorian house, with his flat on the ground floor. Her gaze took in the high skirtings and flamboyant archway halfway down the hall. Around the lights above them, the fittings were ornate.

Carl led them through the kitchen into a large room just ahead of them.

'I'd like to say I've been tidying,' he grinned, 'but, saddo that I am, it was tidy already. Fancy a brew before we get started? The percolator's already on.'

'Anything stronger?' Jade asked, sharply aware of the butterfly wings in her stomach. 'I've had a big meal so I can get away with a small glass of whatever you have.'

Secretly, she was taken aback at her own forwardness, but the need to calm her jittery nerves outweighed any sense of decorum. Carl's grin widened and she caught a tiny glimpse of surprise in his eyes.

'The great Jade Cooke a tiny bit nervous? A turn up, to be sure!' he teased.

'The great Jade Cooke?' she spluttered, placing her red woollen coat onto Carl's outstretched arm. 'Whatever's that all about?'

'You really don't know?' Carl's grin broke into a full smile. 'At work you're known as unshakeable, concrete under pressure, never one to flip out. Whatever Jenny throws at you, you just take it and run.'

Jade laughed aloud at the irony. There she was at work, apparently rock-solid and unyielding, negotiating the whirlwind of an editor with the grace of a kite, yet throw her in front of Carl Heaney for more than two seconds and she was unstable, constantly fighting the urge to surrender, struggling against her loss of control. It was a paradox. Carl made her into a paradox, but she had come here tonight with all her senses on the alert. She knew, more than ever, from the touch of his hand earlier that day, how dangerous things could become and she would erect all her defences to ensure the evening wouldn't prove overly perilous.

She had been given a perfect opportunity to create a great present for Dan — and she wasn't going to let something like this come between her and Brad.

'Well, I'm going to have to shatter your illusions, at least,' she confessed, 'but you don't have to tell the rest of them.' Jade winked, hoping he'd join in the conspiracy.

'Ma's the word,' he replied, placing a finger on the side of the nose Jade had spent so much time admiring that morning.

The strength of feeling that had washed over her back then suddenly revisited and she closed her eyes for an instant, willing the sensation away.

'I never believed it anyway. I knew you were softer than that,' he said quietly.

More words like the words he had gifted her that morning. *We want you safe*, she remembered. *I knew you were softer than that*. They weren't just the words of a colleague from work in conversation and she sensed even more that she was treading on dangerous ground. Civility was being swept aside intermittently and it scared her that these were the words she actually preferred.

'This was the dining room,' he told her, somewhat unnecessarily, 'aka my studio. As you see, I don't do much eating in here.'

Jade looked around, noticing that what looked like the original fireplace had been retained and Carl had adorned it with a companion set of poker, tongs, shovel and dust brush, even though the fireplace itself was closed up.

She knew he had followed her gaze from his next comment that he kept an open fire in the next room and her gaze swept on around the room, observing the chaise lounge and table close by, loaded with a photographer's paraphernalia. She spotted an SLR.

'I remember you said you had a darkroom. I didn't think people bothered with these any more.'

She approached the table, lifting the camera that had caught her eye.

'I don't use it much,' Carl confessed, peeling off his black sweater. Beneath it, he wore a smart white shirt, unbuttoned at the neck and tucked into dark denim jeans. It was a combination Jade would have never have considered, but he passed it off to perfection.

The room was warm and Jade was relieved she wore layers.

'Digital is so much easier and quicker,' he went on, 'but for some shots I still like to use film and develop the images myself. It's odd, I suppose, but it feels more creative. When you see the picture coming to life in the tray, it feels like a type of birth.' He looked at her, surprise lightening the brown of his eyes. 'What an eejit! I've never actually said that out loud before.'

For the first time that she remembered, Jade saw his cheeks redden and it amazed her that something like that would embarrass him. She felt an instinctive urge to reassure him.

'I love that analogy,' she said, messing with the lens of the camera to make him think she hadn't noticed his self-consciousness. 'Perhaps you should write too. I bet you have talent in more than just art.'

Her words hung, tottering in the air, and her breath hung there with them. The innuendo was accidental but she sensed it hadn't gone over Carl's head. She waited to see what he would do with it, whether he would cross the line she'd tried to erect.

'Remains to be seen, I suppose,' he replied, at last puncturing the bubble of stillness.

His response was safely ambiguous and Jade busied herself in relief, moving slowly about the room, closing in on the walls. Each one was filled with unframed, glass-covered photographs and she moved to the left of the fireplace, settling into the alcove, her gaze sweeping over the images arranged apparently randomly.

This wall held many bodies, male and female, some disabled, some fully-abled, clothed or partially undressed, posing for a photographer who obviously celebrated their differences.

Most photos seemed to have been taken ad-hock and Jade's favourite was one of a man, probably in his thirties, leaning out of his wheelchair towards a woman beside him. His hands were placed either side of her face and the intensity of their kiss made Jade's abdomen tingle.

'Fabulous,' she sighed, wishing she had more artistic expertise herself. She was a point and shoot photographer, despite the terminology she had accrued over time, and she could see the way Carl had used background and variations of light to impact on his creations. 'Unusual, too.'

'It's one of my interests,' he said, moving away from the table towards her. 'Highlighting the dissimilarities between us. Showing how life's emotions are shared by all of us whatever our bodies are saying. Photography would be boring if we all looked the same.'

Jade sensed his close proximity and his intense magnetism, attempting to draw her into his space. Wrestling against it, she dragged herself away.

A large sash window broke the next wall up and these photos were of inanimate objects, all from curious angles and hung either side of the window at various heights. Some objects had been superimposed on backgrounds that made the pictures bizarre and she smiled at the effect.

'Clever,' she said. She looked at each one then moved on, keen to see what other themes she would discover, sensing the revelation of a little piece of Carl Heaney in every photograph she beheld.

The far wall was lined with shelves of photography books, magazines and, on the top shelf, twenty or so trophies held pride of place.

'Swimming?' she asked, looking at the ones that were statues. She stood up on tiptoe, trying to see the inscriptions but they were too high up. 'There's a lot of them. You must be very good.'

'Was good,' he corrected, and his tone made it clear that the subject wasn't up for discussion. Nevertheless, she took the risk to continue.

'I used to be a county competitor. What a coincidence.'

Carl's face darkened and Jade knew she should leave it at that. In truth, she was slightly bemused, although strangely buoyed up by the thought of a shared passion, not that it ought to matter.

Images of him in swim shorts brought a slight flush to her chest and she turned back to the pictures, refocusing on why she was there.

The wall behind the door was showered with photos of women. There was no order in their state of attire, some fully clothed here, half-undressed there; but there was something inherantly different about them, something that set them apart from the glamour photos in magazines and it took a while for Jade to work it out.

'No make-up,' she said, triumphantly, peering closely at a shapely young woman, mahogany hair trailing over the back of the chair where she sat.

There was no reddening of the lips or touching up of the cheekbones. Her eyes were a striking blue-grey and Jade marvelled at how, by removing what would have accentuated the eyes and the face, every part of her body became as important as the next. Resting upon her thighs, her hands said far more because the gaze wasn't automatically drawn upwards. Carl had resisted the obvious and in doing so let each part of the woman speak for itself.

'They're very impressive,' she said, realising she still had the camera in her hand. She placed it down on the table.

'Sort of humble.' She paused for a moment, adding, 'The meek shall inherit the earth.'

She looked at him thoughtfully as he made for the door.

'Steady on,' he laughed. 'I'll just go and get that wine.'

Jade continued to look at the pictures, an alarming flash of jealousy sparking through her as she admired the half-naked women confident enough to share their bodies with the world.

She couldn't help but wonder at the intimacy which may or may not have occurred when the photos were taken. *Had any of them been in a relationship with Carl?* she mused, immediately berating herself. Why was she being so stupid? Even if he had, it was nothing to do with her.

Moving away from the powerful images that had disturbed her, she browsed the rows of photography books on the far wall of the room for the few minutes Carl was still gone and, when he returned, she found herself very appreciative of his offering.

As the alcohol seeped into her system, she felt its tentacles searching, stretching, finding every inch of her body. She quickly became more relaxed and welcomed the feeling, having got herself stupidly bothered over some pictures on a wall.

She sipped the wine again, closing her eyes, savouring the sensation of it trickling down inside of her. Being in Carl's personal space, the creative feel of the room . . . there was something about it that inspired her, made her want to be innovative, made her suddenly want to write.

'So, here you go then.' Carl's voice interrupted her sense of solitude and she jumped, looking up from her glass.

'What's this?'

Immediately Jade's calm dissipated into a knot of tension as she saw what appeared to be a damp tissue in Carl's hand.

'Baby wipe,' he replied, matter of factly. 'As effective as make-up remover wipes, just cheaper. Clean it all off and then we can get off the blocks.'

Jade's heart missed a beat but, for a change, the culprit wasn't Carl's gaze. The thought of removing her make-up, especially after having chosen the colours so carefully, filled her with horror. Brad always loved her 'done up' as he put it, the bolder the look, the better. She'd never allowed a guy to see her minus face paint before at least six months into a relationship.

'You're kidding, right?' she said nervously, eyeing her wine. Suddenly, she was unsure that she'd manage the evening on only one glass, searching her purse in her mind's eye to check that she'd have enough cash if she needed a taxi. 'I mean, the photo's for my brother, Carl.'

Carl pressed the wipe into her hand and the touch of his fingers threw her into confusion. Her brain seemed to shatter in all directions, making it impossible to think in a wavy line, let alone a straight one. She sipped some more wine to steady herself, yet it did little to dispel her fear of exposing her features au naturel.

'I know it's for your brother, and he'll love it.' Carl's voice grew gentler until it reached almost a whisper. 'I don't like photographing women wearing make-up. I prefer to capture you as you are, as God made you, not what you want to project to the world . . . Jade . . . ?'

He pressed the wipe deeper into her hand, their fingers still touching, the sound of her name on his lips made her heart sing and, in that moment, she would have done anything he asked.

As she wiped away the painstakingly applied cosmetics, Jade watched his face, darkened with early evening stubble, studying her every move.

By the time she had removed every last bit of lipstick, shadow and powder foundation, she felt as naked as she'd ever felt in her life. Even her day on a naturist beach in Brighton with a previous boyfriend two or three years back hadn't had quite this effect. She had still plastered herself in make-up, despite her body being devoid of clothing, but ironically this was more alien somehow. She passed back the wipe when she'd finished, her hand lingering on his just a split second too long.

'So much better,' he said, standing back to appreciate the overall look. The blackness of his pupils edged out the brown, validating his words. 'Now I can see the real you. Can we take off your cardigan?'

His hands were warm on her shoulders as he began easing it off and Jade passed her glass from one hand to the other as he slid each arm out of its sleeve and then she placed the glass on the table.

'I wish we had natural light,' he complained, 'but there's not much we can do about that.'

He turned off the bulb overhead and Jade saw the standing spotlights, no doubt strategically placed beforehand.

'Do you want me on here?' she asked, moving towards the chaise lounge and, as she turned to him, he regarded her for a long moment. A small shudder of expectation moved through her and she swallowed tightly.

'I certainly do,' Carl replied, with a smile.

He took her arm, his fingers burning through the thinness of her blouse. She allowed herself to be led and then to be seated, surprised to find Carl was suddenly kneeling in front of her, so close she could almost taste the wine on his breath mingling with hers.

'We want you natural, remember?' he reminded her, reaching to the back of her head, his fingers deftly unclipping her hair. The touch of his hand on her scalp made her dizzy and she found herself wishing she had used more clips to secure it that evening . . . anything to extend that contact between them.

Still, he did make quite a meal of it and she suspected that the press of his fingers near the nape of her neck was less of an accident than he made out. The tiny stroke shot a dart of pleasure into her, then he was gone, busying himself with lighting, turning it here, moving it there, adjusting her posture.

Every time any part of their bodies came into contact, she felt the need to reach for her wine. Her resolve was clinging on by its fingernails and she reminded herself of Brad, five hours away, missing her. She tried not to think of the netball team and the inevitable flirting that Brad attracted like moths to a flame.

Jade noticed that Carl used both the cameras, but she preferred the click of the SLR and the winding on of the film. It seemed so much more physical and artistic and, where at first she felt slightly wooden and stiff, Carl had gradually relaxed her with his encouraging words and appreciative sounds.

By the time he appeared to be wrapping up, she had rather got used to hearing his low voice telling her 'yes', 'perfect' and 'brilliant', making her mind race with the mad idea of undoing one or two more of her shirt buttons.

Her mind shot back to the women in the photos on the wall and she looked across at them, wondering how much was real and how much was technologically achieved with Carl's software. What sort of women were they, that some were happy to bare almost all?

Tipping the last dregs of her wine into her dry throat, she plucked up the courage to ask.

'Friends, acquaintances, models . . . all sorts,' Carl replied, flopping down next to her on the chaise lounge. 'Why?'

'No reason.' Jade shrugged, unsure whether to say any more, but the wine had done its job on lowering her inhibitions. 'I just wish I had the confidence to do it, that's all.'

She kept her gaze away from him, looking anywhere in the room other than into his eyes. What on earth must he think of her? Pathetic and needy? Why was she telling him this? Not quite the image she apparently portrayed at work.

'I'm guessing from that, you'd like to

do it?' he asked, his voice wonderfully calming. 'We can take some photos for you, if you'd like. As opposed to for Dan, that is.'

Jade saw the smallest smile playing over his sensual mouth and found it seemed to remove the last of her tension. Her defences were down.

'I guess it seems scary if you've never done it before,' he said, 'but really it isn't. Take a few minutes to think. D'you want some more wine?'

Jade nodded, deciding a taxi home was affordable. If worst came to worst, she could walk.

'Come into the lounge and I can load these images. We could do some photos in there, if you want. It might feel more relaxing.'

Carl picked up the camera, the bottle of wine and then balanced his glass between two fingers. Jade picked up her own glass and followed him up the hall to the next room.

Inside, she was surprised to see the room draped in tinsel and paper-chains, the biggest, most ostentatious tree she'd even seen inside a house dominating the corner beside the bay window. Fairy lights flashed intermittently in the low light.

'Wow!' Jade stood for a moment, transfixed. 'Someone likes Christmas!' A pang of envy, different from the one she felt earlier, dug under her skin. Why couldn't she feel like this?

Carl turned back to look at her. 'Doesn't everyone?' he asked in surprise.

'Not much magic going on there for me. My dad left us at Christmas . . . '

Carl's sigh was dredged from his boots. 'That's a rough one.' For a while he said nothing, his gaze searching her face. 'But there's always magic to find somewhere.' He placed the bottle of wine on the coffee table nearby. 'Perhaps you just have to know where to look.'

Silence hovered between them and she thought of Carl's own kind of magic, casting its spell when they were together. So far she hadn't found a counter spell to defy him — just her own meagre defences that were growing quite weak.

Carl poured them both another glassful then passed hers across. This time their fingers didn't meet and she realised how much she had wanted to touch him again. She slumped into the nearest chair, feeling a little light-headed with the wine.

'Do it,' she said, a sudden euphoria sweeping over her. 'We don't stay the same forever, Carl. Take some pictures that I can keep and look back on when I'm a grey-haired, little old lady.'

She grinned, thinking he'd share in the humour, but in an instant his gaze dropped and he looked totally floored.

'Joke!' she added, attempting to free them both from the uneasiness in the room. 'What I meant was . . . '

What had she meant? she wondered. The sentence remained severed and she waited in silence, until Carl finally spoke.

'You're right, of course,' he said, tossing back half of his wine. 'We don't stay the same, Jade, and some change faster than others. You should celebrate how you are now and, if you change, then you should celebrate again then. We should rejoice that you're here.'

Confused by his meaning and dulled by the alcohol, Jade decided she'd let it go over her head and, buoyed by his slightly manic manner, she began unbuttoning her blouse.

Carl took a step back, once more armed with his camera. 'You're beautiful, Jade. Be confident.'

The camera flashed as together they chose different positions and angles that they could use with her on the settee.

Intoxicated by more than the wine, Jade sporadically undid more buttons until, finally, the pale yellow blouse lay discarded, then the camisole on top of it. The moment she threw herself back onto the settee in her white bra, Carl froze on the spot. He heaved an audible breath, leaning back on the chair by the computer table.

'Wow,' he murmured softly, 'I bet that Secret Santa gift fits a treat.'

Already way past the blushing stage, Jade felt Carl's compliment almost consume her in a wave like a tsunami.

Carl pushed up his sleeves as though he really meant business, exposing his powerful forearms and as she imagined their strength, it made her feel all the more provocative and she thought of the photos they were creating, revealing a side of her that she had, until now, kept hidden.

It felt like giving birth to a hidden part of herself, in the way that Carl had said his darkroom was the deliverer. Carl Heaney, she realised, was the deliverer of an unknown part of herself previously veiled.

He continued to capture the images and, her reserve truly quashed, she relaxed into the game in a way she had never imagined. He continued to shoot, the ultimate professional, and she played to his expertise, throwing herself into the role, although neither was fooling the other.

She could barely breathe for the mutual attraction raging around them, expanding the walls of the room, and she longed for him to lay down the tool of his profession and give in to the storm that she knew was rampant within him as well. Every cell in her body yearned for him to cross the few feet between them and press every inch of his skin against hers.

'Carl?' she breathed, but his 'sshhh' silenced her. He was almost in perpetual motion, as though scared of what might happen if he stopped.

'Carl.'

This time she was more insistent, desire conquering all. What she had feared before she came to his flat had now overtaken her and she saw Carl's arm muscles tighten as he gripped the camera harder than ever, committing her image to something everlasting, now moving closer, then further away.

She knew there was no hiding her awakening, there was nothing left of her hidden, and there never really had been. Carl Heaney was someone she'd never truly been able to hide from and now, half-undressed on his settee, she was exhausted from trying. After months of skirting around each other, months of evasion, she couldn't escape the fact there was something about this man that stripped her right to the core.

Before she knew what she was doing, she was standing before him, his mouth on hers, his hands exploring her back.

The taste of him was sweeter than she had ever imagined, the firmness of his kiss demanding decisiveness in return and she knew she'd not disappoint him. They were matched in their need of the other and she longed for nothing between them as she drank him in, revelling in the deepness of his breathing as his need built.

'If you only knew how long I've waited,' he breathed between kisses, a soft gentleness intermingled with lack of control as if he didn't know quite what to do with her.

Stepping back just a little, she let her hands move up his arms, exploring the muscles, running over his biceps beneath his shirt. His shoulders were broad, broader than Brad's, and she pushed the thought away, too far gone to accept any guilt.

She'd guessed he worked out and then she knew it for sure when she ran her hands over the shirt on his back and his muscles practically rippled under her touch.

Her hunger for him became overwhelming and she drew back again, her fingers a trembling mess as she tried to undo the buttons on his crisp white shirt. She felt like a virgin, muddled and chaotic, but then her hands were all over his chest, tracing his pecs, feeling the tiny tight rise of his belly.

Faintly, almost indistinguishable over their breathing, she heard him murmur her name and she leaned herself against him, tasting his mouth once more. She placed her hands on his shoulders, easing his shirt over them just as he had eased her cardigan over hers what felt like a lifetime ago . . .

In an instant, the atmosphere changed.

Carl withdrew from her sharply, the heat that had been flooding through her freezing under his horrified gaze.

'Don't do that,' he said, shrugging the shirt sharply back over his shoulders and fastening the buttons back up. The blackness of his eyes had receded and they were back to soft, chocolate brown.

Immediately, Jade felt the need to cover herself, jolted into a place she hadn't imagined existed with Carl.

'I'm sorry,' she whispered. 'I didn't mean . . .'

She stopped, unsure what she was saying. She had meant everything she was doing and she'd certainly had the impression that Carl did too.

'What's wrong?' she asked, at last.

Her breath was iced up in her lungs and she was aware once again of the fairy lights flashing on the tree.

Suddenly, she saw the room as it was — the computer desk on the far wall, the flat screen TV in the corner and the white Christmas tree, stylishly adorned with purple and silver tinsel with matching baubles, fairy lights twinkling around the plentiful branches. The impressive open fireplace centred the wall that adjoined the next building; the other walls were festooned with copies of famous art.

She had previously noticed little, blinded by mounting passion, but now it was just Carl Heaney's lounge in his flat and she had undressed herself inside of it, completely consumed by the way she had already known he made her feel.

She felt rather than saw him leave the room as she fumbled for her blouse and camisole then shoved her feet into her shoes.

Tears of confusion welled at the back of her eyes and she fought them, not knowing why they should be there or what even happened.

'I'm sorry, Jade.' Carl's voice was quiet.

He had returned almost as soon as he had retreated and came straight to her side.

She hardly dared look at him but, when she did, a depth of emotion stared back at her that she didn't expect. He opened his mouth to continue but a ringtone pierced into the space around them and he moved to the table and picked up the mobile by the PC. A quick check of the caller failed to deter him from answering and Jade was once more left to her own devices.

Leaving the room, she returned to where she'd left her keys and coat then came back to say she was off.

'Sweetheart, come on, think about what we've been saying,' Carl was whispering intensely into the phone when she paused at the door.

Despite her usual integrity, which she now doubted, she stopped just out of sight, listening for anything more.

'You're beautiful, Annie. Something

special. Look, why don't I call over tomorrow . . . ' she heard Carl saying in his low tone.

Pain wrenching her gut at her stupidity, Jade eased back down the hall and out through the way she'd come in.

Although totally sobered, she realised she still might be over the limit so she grabbed some old trainers from the boot of the car that she kept for walks and tossed her lilac shoes in their place. She made her way home at a run, her brain switched onto auto until she reached her front door, grateful and relieved to have made it unscathed through some of the roads without lighting.

The key couldn't get her in fast enough and she dragged herself straight upstairs and into her familiar bedroom.

Unable to face even a shower, Jade tore off her clothes and fell into bed, ignoring the mobile she'd placed on the table beside her. No way could she ring Brad now, as she'd promised.

Guilt and exhaustion had consumed her and all she could face was the blackness that she hoped would soon overcome it. The wine would help.

She switched off the light, closed her eyes and started to count backwards from a thousand, as she had taught Dan on the nights when he couldn't sleep.

8

It was impossible to believe she had slept at all when the alarm broke into her unconsciousness and Jade cursed it for going off so early.

She drew back the covers, heading for the bathroom, but desperate for more sleep. She felt more exhausted than when she had got into bed in the first place; the intermittent, stress-filled dozing had taken its toll and when she remembered she still had her car to collect from outside Carl's place, the alarm going off early made sense.

Her thoughts were all still a muddled blur and as she pulled open the bedroom curtains, the icy white frost on the roofs all around were almost enough to send her straight back to bed.

She looked longingly at her thick, purple quilt and memory foam pillow, suddenly certain that any sleep she had now would be a million times better than the sleep she'd had throughout the night, and a billion times more refreshing. Surely, if she snuggled back into bed now, she'd feel great in an hour?

But, there was the car. Jade knew that if Jenny sent her out for an interview, she'd be stuffed. She would have to fetch it, no matter how bad she was feeling and, wishing she'd not bothered to look in the mirror, she did her utmost to forget the enormous dark circles under her eyes.

As she sat on the bed lazily pulling her clothes on, she considered the date and how much she'd need left in her account for the rest of the month.

She'd bought pretty much all of her presents, except the frame for the photo, but that wouldn't be much. She could order that online with a charge for next day delivery — assuming she still got the portrait from Carl.

She wouldn't ask for it, that was for sure, and she certainly wouldn't ask

Carl to take her to fetch the car when they were at work, so she picked up her mobile and scrolled the internet for locally based taxi firms.

Fifteen minutes later, a vehicle pulled up outside and Jade climbed into it, grateful for the warmth already pumping from the heater.

The churning of her stomach had little to do with her lack of breakfast and everything to do with her apprehension about meeting Carl. Upon pulling up outside his flat her relief was almost palpable when she found his flat curtains were closed and she paid the driver quickly, keen to get in her car and away as soon as she could.

* * *

Out and about earlier than usual, the traffic in town was quite light and she detoured to the local burger chain, trying to blot out the last time she had been there with Carl. She drove straight into the drive-through with no queue whatsoever and ordered pancakes to go.

The office felt like a different building when Jade arrived. Instead of the usual spark of anticipation, her gaze scanning the room for Carl, she went in, head down, with no wish to see him, or speak.

During her break, her mobile showed a message from Brad but she ignored it, afraid to face even his words on a small screen.

What sort of night had he had?

She thumped the vending machine, not the least bit hungry but in need of something sweet. She remembered the tossing and turning and unruly thoughts, and the machine whirred stupidly, its clutching arm jerking slowly towards her chosen chocolate bar until she felt she was back at the fair as a child, desperate to win the teddy bear prize. Finally it grasped the bar, the thud of its fall seeming to reverberate down the hall.

It was unwrapped and inches from her mouth when Mandy came racing towards her.

'Oh . . . my . . . God! You'll never guess! Jenny's sending me and Carl out on assignment. The leisure centre is upgrading their gym and we're doing a piece on what they're hoping to achieve for the community.'

Jade simply stared at Mandy, clueless how to respond.

'If I'd have known, I'd have worn something different today. Oh, for goodness sake, Jade, why does Jenny always tell us everything so last minute?' Mandy went on. 'What should I say to him, do you think? You know him a bit, don't you? What does he like to talk about?'

Jade's smile was ironic. What did Carl Heaney like talking about? What did he like to discuss? His work. His photos. Jade's brother and what went on in her life. She suddenly realised how much he didn't talk about himself.

Brad talked constantly about his life and what he was doing, what he'd achieved in the past and his future goals.

Looking back to the previous evening,

she couldn't recall having learnt anything new about Carl, bar the swimming trophies up on the shelf, and he hadn't wanted to tell her about them. Despite their apparent shared love of the water, he hadn't wanted to open that door.

There were no photos of him dotted around his flat or any clues to his past. It was as if he had just appeared at the Observer three years ago, having dropped from another universe, and Jade felt a pang of regret that she hadn't probed further, at the same time remembering the wall Carl had erected when she'd tried.

Mandy was messing with her hair in front of the vending machine glass. Well, it was too late now. Jade took a defiant bite of her chocolate bar. There would be no more intimate scenes with Carl Heaney and she felt the trench of shame in her chest when she thought of the pictures he now had of her.

How could she have been so stupid? She swallowed hard and took another huge bite.

'You look amazing as you are, Mandy,' Jade told her, hand over her mouth as she spoke with a mouthful of chocolate. 'What you're wearing is perfect. Just be yourself.'

She studied her colleague for a moment, studying her in a way she hadn't before. Mandy's whirlwind personality was somewhat distracting, but beneath her verbosity, she was a very attractive young girl.

The green dress she wore fitted her to perfection, showing off every curve. She was kind-hearted and always upbeat, if a little self-doubting. She would make a good catch, Jade thought, running her hand down Mandy's arm reassuringly, if only someone would look past her excitable exterior to the cheerful, optimistic woman inside.

One day, Jade thought, as she returned to the office, she would take Mandy Jones to a salon and get them to sort out that unruly hair.

★   ★   ★

Ten minutes later, Jade caught sight of Carl heading in her direction and she immediately grabbed the phone, pretending to take a call.

The reaction was instant. Carl veered off at a tangent, attempting to pass by Mandy's desk but he got caught in her verbal trap and Jade continued to watch him furtively, secretly livid that the sight of him still stirred her to such a degree.

Her fingers trembled on the receiver and she heaved a deep breath to find her equilibrium, trying to whitewash the image of Carl Heaney's skill with the camera and his talent at putting Jade at ease.

She saw Mandy point to the clock and Carl nodded in response then returned to his desk, put something in his drawer and gathered his bag.

Two minutes later, a visibly eager Mandy followed in Carl's wake and Jade's next breath was one of relief.

For the next two hours she found she could almost completely concentrate. She caught up with her writing, tackled her in-tray and visited accounts to sort out a small problem with her pay. A tiny pang of guilt and a large dose of bloody-mindedness over yesterday's lunch-break with Carl drove her to work on through today's lunchbreak and besides, she had little appetite anyway.

At two fifteen, a somewhat subdued Mandy Jones returned, still in Carl's wake. Jade watched Mandy trudge straight past her own desk to the Ladies' out on the corridor, concerned that she looked close to tears.

Carl had disappeared, then suddenly . . . 'Jade?'

'Carl!'

The response was out before Jade had time to think about who had approached her but she was pleased that she had subconsciously managed a tone of rebuke in his name.

Her heart raced from the fright he had given her, apparently having circumnavigated the office to reach her desk from behind, and she leant back against her desk, willing her body to behave. She could do without it freaking out on her — a devil-may-care attitude was what she needed right now.

'What do you want?' she said, when she had steadied her breathing. This time Carl kept his distance, yet his presence still had its familiar impact. He held a large, hard-backed envelope in his hand.

'I brought your photos for Dan. I couldn't decide which was the best so, to be sure, I printed off three to let you choose. They're all pretty stunning.'

Her breath caught in her throat but she refused to let his words get to her.

'That's very kind. So, what do I owe you?' Her tone was completely impersonal, her gaze everywhere but catching his own. She sensed him deflate.

'Don't be like that, Jade. I'm not even going to honour that with an answer.'

There it was again . . . his voice, saying her name, and the effect it always had on her, but she focused instead on the word he had used: 'honour'.

What did Carl Heaney know about honour after that phone call last night? She reached out and took the envelope from him, making it clear she was keen to avoid the touch of his hand.

'Thank you, then,' she said flatly, although she'd rather not have been in his debt.

She looked around swiftly, checking no one was listening in.

'The other ones. I'd like you to delete them.' She wasn't comfortable with them in his possession, not that she thought for a moment he would betray her trust in that way. It's just that she felt so . . . exposed.

'I guessed as much.'

He paused for so long that he cleverly drew her in with his silence and her gaze flipped to him, just for a moment, but that moment was enough.

'I copied them to a CD,' he told her quietly, 'which I've put in the envelope. They're wiped from my PC. You look amazing with make-up, by the way — but mind-blowing without it.'

A flush crept over Jade's neck like a slinky red snake stealing her poise and she blushed still further to know it was there, unsure whether it was Carl's gaze or the thought of her photos in the envelope that had set it off.

'Right,' she managed at last, at a loss to know what to say.

In seconds, the envelope was in her desk drawer in the hope that out of sight would mean out of mind.

Game over, she thought. That's the end of it. But the man who had lately consumed almost all of her waking moments made no move to leave. His hand lingered on the back of her chair and she began to sense him closing in, smelling that same aftershave that provoked intimate memories, recalling the feel of that five o'clock shadow under the palm of her hand.

'Jade, I'd like to explain what happened. It went so unbearably wrong . . . '

'Too right it did!' she exploded, glancing around to ensure her voice had stayed quiet enough, but no one appeared to be even glancing in their direction. 'So, fire away. I'm all ears.'

Her voice was a hiss and she knew she must sound like a fishwife, but the anger burst forth in a wave she couldn't hold back. She folded her arms, waiting for his response and Carl physically withdrew as if stung.

Bingo, she rejoiced in her head, but her celebratory thoughts didn't last long. If Mandy had seemed subdued on her return to the office, Carl Heaney appeared to have taken a near fatal blow. It took him a while to compose himself and she waited again, apprehension creeping steathily through her veins as he seemed to search for the next thing to say.

'Not here, Jade,' he sighed, as if the world had crushed down on him, leaving him breathless. The hand that had ran over her skin less than twenty four hours earlier rubbed nervously at his ear. 'It'd have to be somewhere private.'

His agitation tore at Jade's heart strings and there was something about his sudden vulnerability that made her feel wildly protective.

Frustrated at her own response, she knew she would never be in control when it came to Carl Heaney. She couldn't risk being alone with this unpredictable man any more, if she wanted to save her sanity — or her relationship with Brad.

'Sorry, Carl,' she said, firmly. 'Let's just chalk this down to experience. I appreciate the pictures for Dan, now let's get back to being colleagues where we should've stayed in the first place. I'm with Brad,' she added, to complete the clarification. 'Last night I was way off track.'

Turning her back on him, she held the breath in her lungs until she sensed him move out of her space. She abhorred confrontation and this felt like one of the worst she had ever found herself embroiled in, despite the absence of shouting and screaming.

The look on Carl's face, and his suddenly apparent helplessness contrasting his usual quiet masculine strength, seemed to have scraped out Jade's insides. This time it was her turn to make for the toilets, biting hard on her lip until she reached the sanctity of the cubicle.

Then the tears flowed, unleashing the emotions Carl had stirred in her for much longer than she cared to admit.

Cursing the fact that she hadn't brought in any make-up to refresh herself, she splashed her face and dried herself off, then left the Ladies' with her head high.

Well, you say you like me without any make-up, Mr Heaney, she thought crossly as she strode across the office. *You've got your wish. See what you've jolly-well done.*

9

After the longest afternoon she had ever known in the office, Jade turfed out at five thirty and headed straight for home. She spoke to no one on the way out and avoided Mandy Jones like the plague. It was hard enough dealing with her own feelings about Carl, let alone trying to cope with somebody else's as well. It seemed harsh and wrong for her to behave so selfishly, but it was self-preservation. She needed to regroup and restabilise herself severely, before Brad's return.

She'd only been home ten or so minutes before her mobile rang, the rock band ringtone forewarning her it was Brad. Unable to avoid the inevitable any longer, she answered, the glass of red wine she had already poured held in her other hand.

'Sweetheart. I was getting worried

about you. No texts. What have you been up to?'

Jade swallowed the horribly familiar guilt that rose in her throat. She took a long sip of wine.

'Oh, nothing amazing,' she said, calling on every ounce of energy to inject some cheerfulness into her voice. 'I just went to Mum and Dan's last night to cook them a meal. Dan is so looking forward to Christmas and I can't wait to see him open his iPad.'

Jade stopped, her brain continuing silently with the omission. What she had told Brad so far was all true, but there was much more she wouldn't continue with and, for the first time, it occurred to her that she would have to explain how the portrait came about. How stupid that she had never even thought of it.

'Oh, and I picked up the portrait I had done the other week at the photographers' in town. I never told you about that, did I?' She closed her eyes in a vain attempt to shut out her sense of shame. 'It's for Dan.'

'No, you never said. For Dan, did you say?' Disappointment edged Brad's voice and the line broke up a bit. ' . . . one for me?'

Jade guessed what he was saying, but chose not to respond. She waited for him to ask how her brother was doing, but nothing came.

'I can't hear you very well,' she replied finally, relieved that the conversation was less than flowing. It felt like a get-out clause. 'Did you have a good night last night? How did the team get on today?'

Brad's laughter resounded in her ear.

'They're a wild bunch, that lot. You should've heard some of their stories.'

'I'm sure some were out to impress.' Jade flopped onto the settee, eyeing the fruit, thinking she couldn't manage more than an apple or orange for tea. 'So, did they win?' she asked, suppressing a sigh.

'11-7. They're well chuffed with themselves. The bus'll make its way

back in the morning so I should be
. . . the afternoon. Can't wait to see
you, Jade . . . missed you.'

The cuts in connection were annoying and she wondered how much he
could hear of what she was saying. She
told him a little of her work projects
that day, wishing she could feel his
arms around her, yet at the same time
scared that other arms had been around
him.

It was irrational and she knew it, but
her own indiscretion seemed only to
make it harder to think he'd stayed true
to her when he received so much
attention from other women. She knew
it was wrong to tar him with the same
brush.

'By the way,' she added, remembering a memo from work that she hadn't
passed on to him, 'the management
have said they did reconsider as we
asked but we're definitely not getting a
Christmas 'do' this year. Due to
financial constraints.'

'Oh great!' The irritation in Brad's

voice created a picture of his face in her mind and she almost laughed at how incensed he was. 'People have worked hard all year. They deserve a Christmas 'do'.'

Jade smiled to herself for the first time in the whole conversation. If anyone was going to feel indignant, it was certain to be her Brad.

The possessive in her own thoughts was reassuring and she felt closer to him as a result.

'I can't wait to see you tomorrow,' she said, warmly. 'Shall I come over after work?'

'That'd be nice,' he responded swiftly.

Jade said a lengthy goodbye and hung up, then searched around for something to do. A phone call to her mother didn't help to improve her mood.

'Dan's been playing up today, love,' Linda told her. 'I think the excitement of Christmas has got to him. He's been chucking stuff around and the like.'

Jade remained silent, certain that Christmas wasn't the cause of it, but she knew it wouldn't be wise to launch into that with her mum right now.

'It'll all be over soon, Mum. Just think how occupied he'll be with his iPad. Three days until Christmas. Not long now.'

Fighting the guilt that she hadn't gone over to give Linda a bit of a break, Jade locked the front door and took her wine and an apple upstairs into the bathroom. An hour long soak in lavender bubbles made her feel tons fresher and she eased herself thankfully into bed an hour earlier than she ever remembered managing as an adult.

Exhaustion made every muscle overstretched elastic and sleep came easily for a change. Her book remained open on Brad's side of the bed when she awoke to the alarm in the darkness of a new day.

* * *

Jade was cornered by Mandy as soon as she stepped into the office and immediately did a cartoon double take. For the first time that Jade had ever noticed, Mandy was wearing trousers to work and a smart, businesslike blouse. Her hair was a hot shade of red rather than the mousey brown it had always been and Jade guessed she must have spent the whole of the previous night straightening it. It was silky as a cocoon and almost as long as Jade's hair, which hung way past her shoulders. There was now no need for the clips that her hair had always escaped from and Jade saw that her sparkling eyes were framed with a brown shiny powder and liner to match.

'Good grief!' Jade exclaimed, standing back to take it all in. 'You look amazing! You look so . . . ' She searched for the right word, knowing how important it would be to get it right. 'Sophisticated!'

Mandy blushed down to the spotless new boots beneath her trousers and Jade noticed there were heels where before there had always been flats. In response, Mandy's smile could have powered every PC in the room.

'I don't know what was up with Carl yesterday,' she said brightly, apparently back to her old optimistic self, 'but when I thought about it afterwards, I don't think it was to do with me. I thought he just didn't like me, but when I got home I realised he was upset about something. I don't know why I always have to think that it's all about me.'

Jade looked at her, thinking how such a simple remark showed so much insight. Perhaps if she had thought a bit more about her own outlook on life, she might have avoided some heartache of her own. Her admiration for Mandy took an Olympic-sized leap.

'We ought to go out for a drink sometime in the New Year,' Jade told her suddenly, thinking she had never really bothered to get to know Mandy properly.

She grabbed a post-it note and pen from a nearby desk. Jade had no really close, female friends with so much of her time taken up with Brad, Dan and her mother. It would be good to have some proper girl time, for a change.

'Here's my number,' she said, pressing the note into Mandy's hand.

Mandy's smile broadened further. 'Thanks. That'd be great,' she agreed. 'Perhaps we could eat out as well. Uh-oh, Jenny's out. Hand me a stapler. I'll dump it back on your desk later.'

Laughing at Mandy's overused tactic, Jade passed over her pink and purple stapler, a Christmas tree present last year from Brad. They were her bedroom theme colours and he always made light-hearted fun of her girlie taste.

Mandy scuttled back to her desk in her heels and Jade switched on her PC.

Since she'd arrived at the office, Carl hadn't even glanced up and a sense of relief floated pleasantly through Jade's body, making her feeling slightly light-headed. The day would be infinitely easier if Carl Heaney just kept to himself.

Looking at the screen, Jade noticed an email from Brad sitting patiently in her inbox, apparently sent from his phone on the coach.

There's no place like home. Can't wait to be back.

Jade felt the need to see him over-whelmingly and she strode to the coffee machine, intent on keeping her concentration high and making a huge dent in her workload until he returned.

The plan was successful. The morning passed in a blur with few interruptions, liberating her from compulsive thoughts about what she had done. Even Carl retreated from her mind, unless she looked up.

It was after one pm before she even thought about lunch and she ate as she wrote, distraction returning her appetite just a little bit.

* * *

At two thirty precisely, Brad strode into the office, Harrod's wheelie luggage in tow. Just one more high-status present from Mummy and Daddy, Jade smiled to herself, thinking how lucky it was that Brad's parents lived at the top end of the country.

It was bad enough that they sent him cheques for no reason and bought him all he could ever need; she could only imagine what things would have been like if he'd remained on their doorstep in the Lakes. If they'd known he was in Yorkshire the past couple of days, they'd have been over like a shot.

Jade made her way out into the corridor, not wanting to say her 'welcome homes' in front of everyone in the office and ignoring the small twinge of envy she felt whenever she thought of Brad's mum and dad. What it would be like to have parents who just wanted to take care of you, as opposed to the opposite, it seemed she would never know, but her thoughts were silenced as Brad's arms closed around her, pulling her to his chest.

The corridor was empty and she

rested her head against him, hearing the steady beat of his heart. He smelt good and familiar, lining life into a pleasant symmetry, and the taste of his lips on hers after they'd shared a brief knowing glance was better than she remembered.

It stabilised her, drawing her back to what she knew, and she pushed away the memory of Carl's mouth on hers as each had explored the other. Brad was her guy and she concentrated on him, feeling the firm lines of his body against her as they embraced.

'Nice to have you back, Brad,' came a silky voice from behind them.

The syrupy voice slithered its way between them, its intention totally clear, and the bubble of contentment Jade had found herself in suddenly popped.

She felt Brad's reluctance to pull away, but withdrew he did, and Jade focused her gaze equally reluctantly on Sara Maxwell and her mascara-caked eyelashes as long as her arms. Jade could almost see herself in the gloss on the other woman's lips, the strength of her perfume choking the air.

'Hello Sara,' Brad answered, his hand slipping into Jade's.

I'm hers, she knew he was saying, but her adversary remained undeterred.

'It's been quiet around here without you.'

I've missed you, Jade translated in her mind. 'Funny that,' Jade countered, 'you being in another department.'

Sara eyed her with evident confidence, her response slipping with ease off the snake's tongue.

'Oh, Brad calls in quite often. Don't you, Brad?' Her hand rested on Brad's arm and Jade took a step back towards the office, gently jolting the hand away.

'I bet you've got stacks to catch up on, Brad,' Jade suggested and Brad quickly grabbed his luggage, following swiftly in her wake.

'See you later,' Sara called and Brad rose his eyebrows dispairingly at Jade.

'Uh-huh,' he mumbled, not bothering to look round.

By the time they reached Brad's desk, Jade's disgust had got the better of her.

'Urgh,' she almost spat, 'she just makes me want to . . . '

'Now now,' Brad intervened, laughing, and Jade was spared the regret of putting her dislike into words. His turquoise eyes had lit up in amusement and Jade couldn't help but laugh in response.

'I suppose you're used to it,' she sighed, thinking about the two days and nights of unrelenting attention he would have had from the local netball team.

'Don't let it get to you,' he replied, softly. 'You should be used to it by now.'

He winked and Jade knew he was just trying to lighten the mood, but it did little to reassure her. Was this what she would have to continually live with if they stayed together forever? It wasn't something she wanted to think about right now.

'I'd better get on,' he said, tucking

the luggage under his desk. 'I can't imagine how much I've got to catch up on. I'm interviewing the Yeovil Town manager in an hour. You're coming round tonight, right?'

'I wondered if you fancied popping over to Mum and Dan's with me first? Say hi and play Xbox with Dan?'

Silence met her invitation and she turned away quickly, keen to avoid any confrontation, searching for something neutral to say. Her mind threw up a blank.

'I would, Jade,' Brad finally managed, 'but I've washing and stuff to do. Maybe another night.'

His excuse was feeble but Jade nodded regardless, aware that her smile was less than half-hearted.

Perhaps she was being unfair, she told herself weakly, reassuring him she would be over. It was probably unreasonable to expect him to visit her family on his first night back.

She stubbornly pushed all the previ-ous invitations he had declined to the back of her mind and returned to her article writing with a slightly lower success rate than she'd had throughout the morning. Her concentration wasn't helped by two separate visits from Sara to Brad's desk.

'See you at home later, then.'

Brad's hand squeezed hers as he detoured past her desk on his way out to Huish Park, the Yeovil Town football ground.

Jade had little interest in football but, once he'd left, wished she'd at least asked what the interview was about.

Too late now, she thought, giving him a small wave as he left the office. She could always ask him later, although a small, childish part of her wondered why she should.

Surely it was give and take in a relationship? His interest in her brother was practically nil.

10

At four o'clock, Jade was glad to be sent to interview a man recovering in hospital from an attack the previous night. His condition wasn't critical and she found herself able to interview two family members as well when she was there.

Her journey home took four minutes and she unpacked her work bag, repacked some lunch for the next day and placed it in the fridge.

Upstairs, she glanced at the chair where she had tossed her Secret Santa gift two evenings earlier, deciding she would be leaving it there tonight.

Giving little thought this time to her outfit, she took off her work clothes and changed into jeans and a blue cotton t-shirt, pulling on her favourite angora sweater over the top.

A glass of milk and a bowl of hot

soup later, she was fighting her way through the traffic to her mum's.

'Hey buddy! How's it going?'

Dan was in his usual place in front of the TV and she approached him from behind, having been let in by Linda for a change. Dan was obviously far too engrossed in protecting a random city or something with the biggest guns she'd ever seen, but Jade stopped in her tracks at the sight of her brother from the back. The curvature of his spine to the left was becoming more apparent, his shoulder now far more dipped than the other, and she knew that the scoliosis was getting a hold. The knowledge was like a punch in the stomach and she gathered herself before speaking again.

'Dan?' she said, slightly louder, and he looked around briefly then let out a yell. Before Jade knew what was happening, the Xbox controller was rocketing across the room.

'You made me die!' he yelled in frustration and Jade went to his side to hold onto his hand. A glance at Linda told Jade this wasn't the first time today.

'Time to go out now, buddy boy,' Jade said, asking if he needed a drink or something to eat before they left. The tirade that followed assured her he didn't, so she switched off the television, silently thankful Brad hadn't come with her. He wouldn't have known what to do with himself and she would have been thinking of him as well as her brother. Perhaps, after all, it was easier like this.

Although it was dark, the rain had held off and the winter chill did its job in cooling Dan off. On the flat, he took care of the wheelchair himself, insisting on wheeling it, and she was glad he was getting some exercise

On a rise, she lent a hand and forty minutes passed before they made it back to the house. Secretly, Jade missed the times when she had taken Dan to the park, wishing that he could still manage the monkey bars and get up the slide.

On their return, the house was in darkness and Jade was shocked to find Linda sitting on the settee in the dark.

'Time for homework, Dan,' Jade announced, 'and I'll cook some grub. Rice, veg and grilled fish fingers ok with you?'

'Nice one,' he said, moving straight to his book-bag on the dining table behind the settee.

Linda stirred and smiled at him, but Jade recognised a half-hearted smile when she saw one. She'd provided enough of them herself over the past couple of days and guessing Linda probably hadn't eaten since breakfast, she added extra in the pan to keep up her mother's strength. Obviously, it was a day when her mother's denial wasn't going so well.

'Sorry I killed you off earlier,' Jade told him, once Dan was full after a healthy dinner, 'but you know that's no excuse to lob stuff around the room.' She bit her lip nervously, braced for the potential assault, but was thankful to have gauged the timing just right.

'I know I shouldn't have. Sometimes I just can't seem to help it. It's like something has got inside my head.'

His voice was quiet and so incredibly childlike that Jade thought her heart would dissolve.

She sat down beside him, her arm around his shoulders, feeling now the lean of his shoulder that had started to become so pronounced. She wondered if he had noticed and cursed her own stupidity. Of course he had, she rebuked herself. The boy wasn't blind or insensitive to his own body.

Jade rose to her feet, clearing the condiments from the table unnecessarily early as an excuse to return to the kitchen. She made her mother a hot Ribena, knowing it was her favourite, before taking her leave.

* * *

By now the roads were fairly quiet, the A30 practically clear, and at seven thirty Jade was settled on Brad's settee. Her mood was pretty sombre and she could see that Brad had picked up on it, thinking it was his fault. He tiptoed around her, saying little, making a show of taking the washing from the machine and hanging it all round the flat.

Finally, when he could apparently find nothing more with which to busy himself, he passed her a glass of Baileys on ice and she sipped at it delicately, then placed it on the occasional table in front of her, her attention returning to the TV.

She knew she wasn't being fair to him, but felt too tired to care. It all seemed too much, at that moment in time . . . her brother's illness, her mother's denial, now her phase of being a bit down, which was cyclical.

It came around every Christmas and Jade, of course, knew exactly why.

She reached forward and took another sip of her Baileys, wishing she could get herself into the Christmas spirit like everyone else seemed to manage.

Even Brad's considerable good looks, which were a joy when it was the two of them, had started to get to her after eighteen months of watching girls swarm around him.

The irony was that Brad Wilson wouldn't know a come-on if it hit him in the face, which it frequently did. He was the recipient of more come-ons than any guy Jade had known in her twenty four years and it had taken him forever to ask her out on a date. She daren't try to remember how long she'd had to wait for him to trudge past first base.

Then there was Carl. Her sigh was deep and all-consuming, drifting into the room. Carl-the photographer-Heaney, who had settled himself rather firmly into her consciousness, dominating her thoughts and stealing her sleep.

No, she thought, knocking the rest of her drink back with impressive speed. She couldn't even begin to go there.

'I'm sorry,' Brad said quietly, the settee dipping slightly as he sat down beside her and Jade could barely look at him, knowing her thoughts had been elsewhere. 'I probably should have come with you. I'm always letting you down.'

He edged closer and, although Jade had thought she didn't want physical contact that evening, the arm that slipped around her made her feel wanted and safe. It was all she really needed just now and she allowed herself to lean against him, glad of his warmth and support.

There was nothing she could say about Brad letting her down because she had let him down in a different way. Who was to say which was worse, but neither was good.

She inhaled his familiar, masculine odour, registering that he had showered and not replenished his deodorant. She liked it, that he allowed her to know his real, natural self — a rare occurrence — and the thought was yet one more reminder of what Carl Heaney was about.

Jade closed her eyes, exhausted from

her incessant thoughts, feeling Brad's hand on her arm rubbing her gently. The rhythm was hypnotic and the sensation softly rocked her into oblivion and, at long last, to a much-needed place of escape.

11

Wake up, Jade. It's half seven.' Brad's voice filtered through Jade's state of semi-consciousness and she forced open her eyes, certain each lid must be laden with lead.

The sleep-blurred focus confused her at first and she wondered where her pink and white starry curtains had disappeared to. Instead of her thick, purple winter duvet, she was covered by a heavy black quilt covered with racing cars. Despite her exhaustion, a weak smile pulled at the corners of her mouth.

'What are you? Five?' She eased herself into a sitting position, wondering why she was dressed.

'Uh?' Brad's brow creased in confusion.

'Racing cars? Don't most guys of twenty eight have half-naked women on their quilts?'

Brad's shoulders rose in an easy

shrug. 'It's my spare.' He smiled briefly then passed her a steaming mug of coffee. 'You might want to shower first before you drink it. It's a bit hot.'

'Thanks.' Jade took it from him, her knuckle burning against the ceramic. 'Have I been here all night?'

Brad nodded. 'You were out like a light and I didn't want to disturb you. You've got some spare clothes in the drawer. There must be something clean in there you can wear for work.'

Now it was Jade's turn to nod. She flipped herself off the settee, knocking the quilt to the floor. No pack-up for lunch, no make-up. All she could do was shower to freshen up and she did it with speed and then faced Brad's homemade healthful cardboard muesli breakfast.

She was grateful to find a tatty old eyeliner chucked in the drawer with her clothes and she used a spot of Brad's Dove for Men moisturiser with more than a little amusement. For a guy who used so many products, he was fascinatingly unaware of the effect.

Even his spray deodorant smelt pretty good on her and she thought she would enjoy it herself until it faded later in the day.

When she picked up her bag, she thought of her packed lunch in the fridge back at her own house. For the first time ever, she would have to buy from the woman who came round with sandwiches and baked goods during the morning — something she'd always quite fancied but couldn't usually justify the expense. Oh well, a Christmas indulgence, she thought as she and Brad left the flat together.

Each climbed into their own car after Brad's peck on the cheek and it seemed a little ridiculous, both headed in the same direction to the same place, but they would be headed their own ways after work so there was no point in pooling cars.

She parked a few spaces from Brad in the multi-storey, glad to leave the car and the persistent Christmas music. It didn't matter what radio station she chose, it popped up unrelentingly.

They entered the office together and Jade remembered how they would once have held hands from the car park, dropping hands at the office double doors. Now, Brad entered a few paces ahead of her and she'd had to keep up as they'd ascended the stairs from the car park. They never took the lift if they came in together — Brad would have freaked out at just the thought.

The room was bustling and Jade sensed the air of tension as staff bustled about, trying to get ahead as the Christmas break loomed.

In no time, she had her head down, doing the same. The idea of time off always seemed fab, until she got into the office and remembered what it would do to her workload.

★　★　★

She was flat out all morning and it was a near miss when the sandwich lady appeared and had almost gone again before Jade even noticed her. She darted across the room to the door where the tray was and was peering at the labels when something intangible dragged her mind from what she was doing. Whatever it was had returned her swiftly to three nights ago.

'Are you off to the Christmas 'do', then?'

The Irish accent brushed over her with the softness of a feather and Jade inhaled the delicious muskiness of Carl's aftershave that she now knew so well. He was leaning over the tray alongside her, pretending to be choosing a sandwich but Jade knew that he usually brought his own lunch.

The sandwich lady picked up the tray, ready to move on to the next deparment on their floor.

'Oh, excuse me. Sorry. Could I have a tuna mayonnaise?'

Jade grabbed one from the tray, willing her fingers to stop trembling. How would Carl not see what a state she was in? The change in her pocket had a life of its own and she cursed under her breath when it leapt from her hand and scattered all over the office floor.

Before she knew what was happening, Carl was down on the floor with her, scrabbling around for coins on the brown patterned carpet.

It didn't help the situation much. His close proximity was completely disarming, giving her the confusing sense of both wanting to move closer and wishing he'd leave her alone.

Her body froze as if hit by a chill, goosebumps broke out all over and Jade pushed herself unceremoniously to her feet, the chill soon thawing to fire on her cheeks as she accepted the money Carl had collected. Jade counted out two pounds twenty five and passed it to the sandwich lady patiently waiting nearby.

'The 'do'? Will you be going?' Carl repeated, as if nothing had happened between his last sentence and this.

'What 'do'?' Jade retorted, sharply. How many times did this man have to upset her equilibrium? The memory of leaving Carl's place with him on the phone to some other woman toughened her stance. And, anyway, what was he on about? There was no Christmas 'do' this year. The recent memo had told them that.

'Well, Brad's been organising it for the past hour. I thought you'd have known.'

Suspecting a smidgen of teasing in his voice, Jade bristled still further, unfairly angry with Brad for putting her on the back foot, but he'd never mentioned anything that morning about arranging a staff Christmas get-together.

Determined not to look completely out of the loop, Jade looked Carl straight in the eye, immediately wishing she hadn't. She had the sense he could see right through her.

'Of course I'm going,' she lied. 'Aren't you?'

'Possibly.' Carl eyed her with a sly

grin on his face. 'I'll see how I feel later. Where are we going again?'

Jade sensed the game he was playing. Well, she could play it as well. She opened her sandwich nonchalantly, praying she wouldn't get mayonnaise all over herself.

'I don't know yet. He was going to ask people where they fancied and see which was the most popular.'

'Ah, really?' Carl's Irish lilt came to the fore as he leant, equally nonchalantly, on the table beside her where the sandwich box had been. 'That's odd 'cos he told me it was 'spoons'.' The victory showed as the smallest glint in his eyes.

Jade smiled sweetly, refusing to be drawn in to a battle of who knew what. She turned, as if to move off.

'Might see you later then. If I make it.'

Oh damn it, that accent, Jade cussed, realising how the sound of his voice was affecting her more and more each time they spoke. It had kind of crept up on her but, of course, Carl now knew the effect he was starting to have on her. She'd found it impossible to control herself when they'd been alone in his flat and he was entirely too dangerous to be around. She needed to keep her distance if she was to have any chance of hanging on to her sanity. Carl Heaney had the potential to drive her completely insane.

Nevertheless, and despite all that she'd told herself, Jade spent most of the afternoon in a dither, trying to get her desk cleared and her articles finished but drifting off into a dream. She knew she should show some good sense, she should exercise better judgement, but her mind skipped ahead to the Christmas outing that evening and created all sorts of x-rated scenarios, each one starring the man she was supposed to be keeping away from. Contrary to what she had decided, she longed for him to turn up after all.

12

The temptation to put on her Secret Santa gift was almost too much. Tossed onto the bed beside her little red dress, Jade glanced at it one time too many, wondering again if it had come from Brad. It was impossible to know as he would never let on. She'd seen him hide a receipt a week ago in the kitchen and he'd joked that she should 'keep her nose out'.

'A secret's a secret, after all,' he had said. 'Where's the fun if you tell?'

But they'd had no fun with it so far. The only fun Jade had had with her present had occurred in her mind. So many imagined situations had stirred her into a frenzy and, intent on not letting herself go there again, she shoved the lingerie into a drawer, knowing it was even worse to be fantasising about something with one man, wearing something that came from another.

She put on a pair of silk camisole knickers instead and matching bra. They were flowery and feminine and she loved their softness next to her skin, making her feel different to the Christmas lingerie.

When she pulled the red dress over her head and did up the zip, the material clung to her, accentuating her shape, and it was a shape that she hid at work under her office clothes. Pleased with the result, she turned to her dresser, finding herself looking for more neutral colours than usual.

Brad liked the bright red of her evening lipstick and the bolder shades for her eyes, but tonight she brushed her eyelids with a soft beige-brown with chocolate liner. Her lips stayed their natural colour, rolled with a cherry gloss. A skin-coloured powder with no foundation seemed quite enough and her mascara was barely detectable.

It was strange but she had begun to

think Carl was right with his 'less is more'. Her real self was shining right through.

She picked up her pearl flower-shaped hair clip and brushed her hair upwards into a bun. Stray strands refused to play the game and it took two or three minutes to secure it as she checked it was all in place.

Her lace-top stay-ups on, Jade slipped on her black heels then, satisfied she was ready, returned to the full length mirror, twisting this way and that, regarding herself with a critical eye.

The straps of her shoes crisscrossed symmetrically, emphasising her slender ankles, and her gaze rose over her thighs to the pinch of her waist and up to her chest. She was certainly in proportion and she continued to assess herself objectively, her gaze continuing over her neck to her face and her hair.

Something didn't quite gel. It took a while but she finally saw the problem. Her hair made her look like something out of a movie so, reluctantly undoing the clip she had painstakingly added, her long dark auburn hair tumbled softly in waves onto her shoulders, down onto her chest. She brushed down the length of it for a minute, then sprayed it with spray gloss and, this time, her reflection said she'd got it right.

Stubbornly ignoring the fact that she'd thought only of Carl's reaction when she'd dressed, Jade took her black Jaeger Claudette clutchbag from a drawer, which only ever came out on special occasions. Special occasion — a work's Christmas party? Who was she trying to kid? She quickly threw her phone and purse inside and was just stepping out of the door when her mobile rang.

'Mum? Is everything ok?'

A lurch of guilt hit her as she realised she'd been too preoccupied to even think of ringing her mother. The guilt combined with panic as she imagined a million different reasons why Linda had rung.

'Fine, love. I just thought I'd give you a ring and say that Dan's had a good day. He had a friend round after school and they seemed to have fun on the Xbox. The lad stayed for tea and hasn't long gone.'

'That's fantastic, Mum.' The relief washed down Jade's guilt. 'Thanks for ringing to tell me. You've made my day. And how are you?' Jade added, trying hard to disguise her hesitation, dreading the response.

'Oh, I'm fine, sweetheart. I cleaned through the house this afternoon when Dan had his friend over. Sort of gave me a lift.'

Jade sighed quietly with relief. 'I'm sorry I didn't ring,' she said, fingering the key in her hand, thinking how she should have taken just a few minutes to ring home earlier. 'It's been a bit manic, what with Christmas coming and that.'

No excuse, she told herself silently but, nevertheless, the call ended on a higher note than Jade could have hoped, having told Linda she was out at

Wetherspoons tonight.

'Good. You deserve some fun, girl. Enjoy yourself. If I don't see you tomorrow, we'll see you on Christmas Day.'

This time Linda was first to press the cut-off button and Jade held the phone to her ear for a few more moments, thinking how good it was to go out tonight reassured that things were well at home. It was as though a weight had been lifted and, although she knew tomorrow may be different, she would make the most of it while it lasted and literally let her hair down for the night.

Shrugging on her black knee-length coat, she stepped outside and locked the door behind her, placed her keys in her bag and strode on past the car. It was an advantage of living so close to town, she always told visitors, and if she wasn't required to go out for interviews at a moment's notice, she would have walked to work too.

The sharp air gave her a second wind and she strode energetically over the crossing as the man turned to green, making her way down Wyndham Road and into the town centre.

Wetherspoons was heaving and she pushed her way through the throng, searching for faces from the office. She didn't expect to see Brad first but there he was, Sara Maxwell practically hanging onto his arm. The sight pierced the tiniest hole in Jade's bubble, enough for it to deflate, but she gathered herself up and moved to Brad's side, putting her arms around him.

'Hey,' she said, loud enough to be heard over the conversational drone.

'Hey, you made it! Wow, your hair's down.'

It was impossible to tell from his tone whether or not he liked it and Jade found it a little disconcerting. There was no comment as to the rest of her . . . the red dress that clung to her figure, her elegant shoes. Brad pecked her on the cheek lightly then looked around the room.

'The others are here somewhere.

Aren't they, Sara?'

Sara shrugged noncommittally, as if she couldn't care less.

'Somewhere,' she purred, and Jade read so much more into Sara's one word.

She took in the girl's attire, unsurprised to discover a short skirt and blue sequinned top that was out of the eighties, skin-tight and low cut. Her hair was bleached blonde, tied in a ponytail and swinging like a cheerleader from the US; at twenty-one, Sara still acted like she was a teenager.

Above the buzz, Jade realised that Brad was offering her a drink and she turned back to him, thinking how handsome he looked. He wore faded jeans with a cut-sleeve T-shirt she recognised, topped with a jacket from one of the trendier clothes stores they'd been to in Cribbs. Every now and again, they would shop together in Bristol and it was one day out Brad always loved. They'd lunch in the big food hall then spend the day browsing, trying and buying.

Jade's friends were always so envious that she had a guy who adored shopping, but Jade didn't always find it as remarkable as they imagined. When Jade was collecting clothes she wanted to try on in the ladies' stores, Brad would make all the right noises, but she always felt that he couldn't wait to get back to the section with the bloke's stuff. It was more relaxing to shop alone.

'Drink, Jade?' Brad repeated and Jade nodded her thanks.

She guessed that the glass in Sara's hand had been egged out of Brad and made a mental note to ensure she returned the favour to Brad later. She never took advantage of a bloke, unlike some, she thought, eyeing the girl beside her. Brad was easy to take advantage of, chugging through life, never really seeing much beyond his own little world.

She watched as Brad wove his way through the drinkers to the bar then turned to Sara whose gaze was glued to

Brad's backside.

'Doesn't it bother you,' Jade said lightly, 'that he already has a girlfriend?'

To her credit, Sara kept her cool, looking Jade straight in the eye.

'Not really,' she shrugged, her blue eyes clear as a polished diamond and Jade found herself secretly admiring such honesty. At least there was no pretence with Sara Maxwell. What you saw was most definitely what you got and she went after what she wanted with no holds barred.

'All's fair in love and war,' Sara said, her moist, scarlet lips closing around the straw of her cocktail. She sucked on it for a moment then added, 'You two aren't right together, anyway.'

'Really?' Taken aback, Jade kept her voice steady regardless. 'And what makes you say that?'

The song banging out of the speakers, changed to another with a faster bass, making it harder than ever to hear. She leant forwards, into the environs of Sara's perfume, almost overwhelmed by its potent aroma.

To Jade's surprise, Sara looked thoughtful for a moment, giving the question more consideration than she had expected. Finally, Sara replied. 'I dunno, to be honest. I just think there's no . . . spark. Nothing you can pick up on really . . . Sort of brother and sister.'

Indignation caught Jade unawares and she could no longer remain objective. She looked over at Brad who was now being served at the bar.

'That's ridiculous,' she almost shouted above the din. 'We're different in the office. You can't go round at work holding hands, kissing each other all the time,' but Sara stayed calm, winding Jade up even further. She took another long sip of her cocktail before countering Jade's denial.

'Ah yes, but you can't hide it when it's there. You're disconnected, the pair of you. Yes, disconnected. That's it.'

Jade's composure flew out of the window as Sara's composure frustratingly seemed to grow.

Out of the corner of her eye, she saw Brad approaching with her drink and she wanted to get the last word before he arrived.

'You don't know anything about us,' she blurted, childishly, at a loss as how to counter the argument.

What did she know? Jade thought angrily, but as she grappled for a response that would put Sara in her place, she failed miserably.

Disconnected.

The word stuck with her and she glanced down at herself, troubled that Brad hadn't even remarked on how she looked, except for the change in her hairstyle. But then he wouldn't have noticed Sara's get up, either. It was just the way he was wired.

'Thanks, Brad,' she said, accepting the gin and tonic. She smiled at him but he was looking at the door.

'I don't think everyone's here yet. I've been keeping an eye on who's come in.' He stretched up on tiptoe to peer over some heads, being two or three inches shorter than some.

'Well I'm off to find out who is, then,' Jade announced, glancing around the masses. 'I'll leave you two to it,' she added pointedly, looking directly at Sara, who just smiled, chilled as a bear in the Arctic, her painted nails ready to snare their catch.

Jade left them, pretending that she was just searching generally, but with only one person in mind. She looked around the tables, at the bar, at the edges of the room and drew a blank. Then again, he hadn't actually said that he was coming, she remembered. *If he made it*, he'd said. She smiled at a few colleagues loitering around in small groups then made a beeline for the Ladies'.

Placing her drink next to the sinks, she headed for an empty cubicle but, before she reached it, Mandy Jones stepped out of one near the end.

'Oh, hi Jade!'

Her tinkly voice was laced with high spirits and Jade almost took a step back, still unused to Mandy's new look. Tonight she looked dazzling in a pastel-blue dress, drawn in at the waist with a slim, shiny black belt. Pastel-blue eye shadow complemented the dress, and long dangly sapphire earrings with a necklace to match. The sapphire hung just above an impressive cleavage, drawing attention to her feminine charms, and Jade thought Mandy had never looked quite so stunning. Even her new business-like office gear had not been a contest for this.

'Have you found yourself a personal shopper, Mandy?' Jade joked.

To Jade's genuine dismay, Mandy became flustered.

'Is it too much?'

Her hot red hair shone beneath overhead lights as she nervously smoothed down her dress.

'It might be a little too much for some but not in the way you're thinking! You look gorgeous.' Jade laughed, leaning against the sink and wishing she hadn't. She felt a wet line appear just above her backside. 'Urrrgh,' she complained. 'Why does everyone make so much mess at the sinks?'

'Here. Turn round.'

Mandy guided Jade backwards towards one of the dryers and Jade shuffled along, giggling as she tripped and almost fell.

'Stop!' Mandy instructed with surprising authority, and Jade felt the jet of hot air hit her back.

Mandy had twisted the nozzle so that the stream headed downwards and her hand eased Jade's dress material away from her body so that the heat would dry it off quicker. Silence settled between them as the dryer's whir killed any attempts at conversation. Such a simple action felt surprisingly intimate and Jade sensed she was with a friend more than a colleague, glad that she had bumped into Mandy like this.

Lately, whenever they had spoken or interacted, her respect for Mandy had increased. It was as if she had kept herself hidden under her verbosity and Jade was beginning to really like what she saw. She could imagine them being good friends and was more determined than ever that they should spend time together in the New Year.

'I don't suppose you fancy a shopping trip when the sales start?' Jade asked, suddenly filled with an inspiration when the dryer halted abruptly. 'Looking at you these last couple of days, I think you could give me a lesson or two!'

Mandy flushed with what Jade hoped was pleasure, her hands fiddling with her handbag. She tucked it under her arm and leant carefully over the basin, learning from Jade's mistake.

'That'd be fun!' she replied, scrubbing her hands under the hot tap. 'We'll have to make a date.'

'See you out there in a minute,' Jade said, making her way to the cubicle.

By the time Jade emerged a couple of minutes later, Mandy was scrutinising a menu at a table, chatting with Les from accounts and Jade smiled, pleased to see her so happy.

Mandy seemed to have come to life recently and Jade wondered at the change, but her thoughts didn't have long to dwell on it as her heart almost went into arrest.

Carl Heaney was headed straight for her and she swallowed the dryness in her throat then threw back a huge mouthful of gin and tonic. He exuded determination and she stood, rooted to the spot, prey frozen in fear at the sight of its predator.

13

Jade braced herself, waiting for the onslaught, confused as to what it might be because Carl Heaney looked angry, his jaw tight, hands clenched at his sides.

He stopped a few feet away, appearing about to say something, his eyes blazing with an emotion she couldn't quite fathom. He had her well and truly in his sights, close enough to reach out and touch her, and the urge to touch him overwhelmed her as she longed to take his anger away. The yearning to make him feel better confused her as she recalled how he had made her feel just a few nights earlier, turning her on then blowing her out. She remembered his shoulders under her hands, the smoothness and the strength of them, then his rejection as he shook her away.

Now, Jade felt his brown eyes drill

into her, seeming to pull her thoughts out into the open and then, as fast as he'd arrived, he was gone.

Jade was in no man's land, unfamiliar terrain, having just evaded fire. The stress of it made her dizzy and she edged towards a nearby pillar, her gaze fixed on the door Carl had barged through. Surely he'd come out and finish what he'd started? But she waited in vain, scrabbling for stability in the heat and noise all around her.

Focus, she told herself, looking for something to distract her . . . a menu from the bar. They were eating at eight, in just over five minutes, and she knew Brad had checked there'd be room, so she didn't have long to survive. The distraction worked for about twenty seconds as she looked over the choices, but her thoughts soon boomeranged back.

How dare he freak her out like that? she raged inwardly, her hackles as high as the clock tower at the far end of town. Who the hell did he think he was, charging up then storming off, making her look totally stupid? The man was just too unpredictable. Brad she could read like a book. Steady and stable was what she needed, not a guy who turned life into a rollercoaster from hell. Fair enough, Carl Heaney might also be offering a little bit of heaven along with it, but life was already too erratic for Jade to purposely add any more variables.

She watched the staff move tables, arranging cutlery, setting a column of red and gold decorations on top. Brad had gone out and bought paper hats which he now placed on each and every setting and Jade watched him, amused at how meticulous he was. Each hat had to be right in the centre of each setting, a serviette triangle beneath it, and it made her think of his kitchen, where everything had its place.

She had once decided to cook for him at his but, after the fuss he made over how she'd put things away after-wards, she'd never bothered again. Now she could see he was in his element, buzzing around, organising everyone into their places.

She was sat opposite him with a bloke from accounts on her left and Simon Black, Deputy Editor, on her right, and she placed her glass dutifully in front of her hat, relieved to see Carl was way down the table nearest the door. Brad was flanked by Mandy Jones on one side and Hannah Hawkins from advertising on the other. All in all, she had to admit, not a bad mix.

★ ★ ★

The food was with them by eight twenty and they'd vacated the tables by nine forty-five. The rowdiness had increased disproportionately to the time that had passed and most had gravitated into groups and couples.

Jade had found herself chatting with Simon about how nationwide cutbacks affected their paper. Brad was propped up against one of the pillars with

Mandy, pulling apart the government's most recent proposals on preventing obesity.

Jade bought him a beer and took it over, taking a while to catch his attention. The conversation was apparently gripping and she practically shoved the glass into his hand before he even knew she was there.

'You can't put it all down to the government,' he was saying earnestly. 'Parents have to learn to say no.'

'Well, when you're a parent, you'll probably find out how tough it is,' Jade interjected, and both faces turned together.

All of a sudden, she felt the outsider and wished she'd kept her thoughts to herself. The word 'parent' fell like a lead weight between her and Brad and she was knocked flat by the knowledge that never quite left her: would she even be able to have kids of her own, as a potential carrier of Duchenne Muscular Dystrophy? She saw the same thought rushing through Brad's mind. It was something he refused to discuss.

'It's got to be a joint effort, I think,' Mandy interceded, her glance moving slowly from one to the other, assessing the situation and drawing Jade back from an emotional brink.

The few drinks she'd had were affecting her more than usual, probably due to her recent lack of sleep and, secretly, Jade thanked Mandy for her tact, leaving them to it.

Jade did the rounds for a while, joining in with the odd overheard discussion that sounded of interest, but avoided any group that involved Carl.

At around ten thirty, a group of men from the office caught her attention and she laughed as she heard music from *The Full Monty* come on. The guys were pulling others in with them, encouraging them to start stripping off and, having downed more than was probably good for her, Jade gradually joined in with the chanting. The men had put on ties and were slowly undoing them, swinging their hips, all quite obviously premeditated. The DJ seemed to be in on the act and Jade caught Carl's eye a few metres away as he hung in the background, looking thoroughly out of sorts.

He looked away, suddenly intent on examining the beer-stained carpet and Jade found the gin taking control.

'Come on, Carl.'

Jade grabbed his arm, putting all her might into dragging him out to the others. She could feel his forearms tense up against her and a memory of how he'd looked with his sleeves rolled up swept through her mind. How she longed to see that again, and more besides.

'It's not my thing,' Carl said sharply, shrugging her off, but the slight buzz of drunkenness made her persist.

'Come on,' she urged, looking him straight in the eye, 'what are you afraid of? You can more than give them a run for their money. Your body's better than all their best bits put together.'

Jade bit her tongue, but it was too

late to try and cover up what she'd said. It was out there in the open and she continued to look at Carl, expecting a certain smugness, but it was a long way from what she saw. His face had clouded like thunder and he jerked his arm away so roughly, it almost yanked her own out of its socket.

'That's all you care about, is it?' he said cruelly, looking around the room. 'That's all anyone seems to care about nowadays. It's all about what you look like. Well, Jade, there's a lot more to me than that.'

In an instant, he had disappeared into the crowd at the bar.

By now, the whole place had come to a standstill watching the dancefloor show that had progressed quite dramatically, and Jade stood with a heavy heart, no longer enjoying the performance as she had. Some of the guys were down to their underwear and the music was coming to a close.

She knew, like everyone, what happened next and looked across to see what Brad was making of the routine. Jade had seen he'd not taken part and wasn't the least bit surprised, but what she'd missed was that he was not even aware of what was happening. So engrossed was he in his conversation with Mandy, pink aliens could have landed and he would have just nodded as they passed.

There was something about him, something she'd never noticed before, and she stared for some time, trying to work out what it was, but it kept on eluding her.

Finally, it struck her, but she realised that it wasn't so much that she'd never noticed it . . . more that she'd never seen it before. Brad was lounging against the pillar, like so many other guys in the place, and the truth was, he was like them in a way that was foreign to Jade. Every fibre of Brad's being was relaxed in a way Jade had never known — at least, not unless he was left to his own devices, in Brad's own little world.

It was as if Mandy had climbed into

Brad's world with him, or maybe he had climbed into hers. There were no explosive fireworks, like Sara Maxwell seemed to think ought to be shooting all around them, except maybe the slow whirr of a colourful Catherine Wheel creating its own distinctive pattern.

Jade watched them mirroring gestures, invading each other's space with an ease it would usually take time to achieve, then saw Brad become suddenly animated. He reached out and touched Mandy's arm, but neither seemed to perceive the crossing of a boundary.

Jade turned back to the show, unsure quite how it was making her feel.

All at once, she was aware of a commotion, with her colleagues trickling into the centre of the room. Simon, Terry and Kev had apparently gone the whole hog and whipped off their boxers with merely a serviette to cover their blushes. Jade couldn't help but laugh, despite her clash with Carl, but the bar staff didn't share in the joke. Before two minutes were up, they were out on the street. Mandy and Brad were two of the last to trail out of the pub.

'What's going on?' Brad asked and Jade heard Jenny Jackson explain through her laughter.

Jade looked around for Carl, thinking he'd have left, but there he was, in the background, as ever watching on as Kev tiptoed up Middle Street, cheeks as pale as the hazy moon above, yelling, 'Back to mine!'

Jade smiled as the pack traipsed after him like drunken rats trailing the Pied Piper. A few had taken their glasses with them, upset at being kicked out and she couldn't help thinking that Kev wouldn't consider his idea quite so enthusiastically when faced with his place in the morning.

A few veered off to the supermaket to get some supplies and the others ploughed on to Crofton Park.

Kev's place was on the ground floor in a shared house and someone went round inviting the neighbours, in hopes of keeping the peace.

His room was strewn with tinsel and Christmas paraphernalia and Jade had an uncomfortable sense she was the only person on earth who never bothered with decorations.

Had Scrooge been a newspaper reporter, Jade thought, *then he would have been female and called Jade Cooke.*

When the beers arrived, Jade tucked a tenner into a bowl and broke open a seal, thinking how she really ought to go easy now, but was somehow past caring. Not much of a drinker generally, she'd been knocking them back a bit rather, of late.

Brad and Mandy were on the settee, still deep in conversation, hands inches from each other, the rest of the room appearing shut out.

'At least someone is feeling at home.'

The voice was unmistakeable and Jade let the soft lilt drift over her before turning to face Carl.

14

'And you're not?' She was relieved to see that his anger had dissipated but the warning light flashed red at the back of her mind. Hadn't she just told herself that this man was dangerous and wasn't she still livid at how he'd treated her at the pub? But the beer had made everything softer and she waited for him to respond.

'Getting there.' He smiled and she despaired at the way it jump-started her pulse. 'I'll be there by the end of the night.'

Jade was tempted to ask what he meant, but thoughts of their heated exchange crowded her mind and she felt indignant. She couldn't just leave what he'd said earlier without putting him straight.

'You've got me all wrong, you know,' she told him, drawing in a deep breath to brace up her courage. 'I'm not all about looks. You seem to think that I'm superficial and, to be honest, that makes me mad.'

'I know, Jade.' The soulful brown eyes that had held her gaze now darted away momentarily then returned just as fast. 'Look, let's just forget it. I just wanted to ask you, have you chosen which portrait you're going to give to your brother yet?'

Jade felt the blush of ingratitude stain her cheeks as she thought of the envelope still in her workbag.

'Not yet,' she confessed, thinking that at least she had remembered to grab them from her desk drawer before the office had closed for Christmas. 'To tell you the truth, Carl, I haven't looked at them. Not after . . . not after the other night, but I'm waiting for a frame to arrive in the post. It'd better get here tomorrow or I'm stuffed. Well, at least Dan'll have his iPad. The portrait's a bit of an extra.'

She realised she was waffling and

Carl looked blank.

'I can't hear you!' he said, raising his voice above the music that had been cranked up pretty fast. 'Come out here!'

They moved from beside Kev's speaker and Jade glanced back at Brad before leaving the room. He was still engrossed in conversation, his head thrown back in laughter and Mandy the same, but their bodies weren't touching.

A dart of something intangible flashed through her as Carl's hand slipped into her own and he led her from the room on what felt like a potential adventure. Once the door was shut, the buzz in Jade's ear from the noise, coupled with alcohol she wasn't used to, made her lean back on the wall.

'I've had enough to drink,' she sighed. 'I don't want any more. I just want some water.'

She put her beer can on the floor, suddenly sick of the smell. This just wasn't her, drinking alcohol every night, and she wanted her head back, bright and clear like it used to be. It only added to her exhaustion, apart from anything else.

'Wait here,' Carl instructed and strode off down the hall. In a moment, he was back with a glass filled with chilled water and Jade downed it in two.

'Easy,' Carl told her, taking the glass and resting it on the banister nearby. 'We don't want you drowning,' he laughed.

Little did he know, Jade thought to herself, that she was already way over her head, and he was the cause. She closed her eyes, hearing the slow thump of the music now dulled by the closed door, and swayed gently against the wall, the tiredness starting to claim her. If she could sleep standing up like a horse, she'd have done it by now.

'I liked the photo of you looking slightly askew at the camera. For Dan, I mean. To frame for your brother.'

Jade slid down the wall and sat on the laminate flooring. From there, Carl looked like some kind of giant and her gaze rose up his body, taking in his thighs in his navy chinos. His pale blue shirt hung, untucked, at his hips and she counted the buttons that closed off the taut, powerful stomach she had recently felt under her palms. How many could she manage to open, she wondered airily, before Carl's hands would bring her to an unwelcome halt?

The water was beginning to re-energise her just a little, but she liked the sense of respite she was getting down on the floor. A couple burst out of the door and brushed past Carl holding hands. Jade's abdomen clenched at the rise of Carl's eyebrows.

'Jenny and Martin,' he mouthed, with a grin.

Lucky them, Jade thought, despite her resolve.

'So, I liked the one of you looking slightly side on. You'll know which one I mean when you look at them. The others are pretty good too, though I say it myself.'

The others, Jade thought hotly, resuming her carnal examination of Carl's form. His voice echoed inside her head — *there's more to me than what I look like* — but it didn't deter her. She knew he could see she was looking and it fed her wantonness even more. By the time she had reached the soft spiky hair at the crown of his head, the urge to run her fingers through it propelled her to her feet and she reached up to touch it, her fingertips brushing it gently.

Carl laughed, grabbing her hand equally gently, complaining about how long it had taken him to get the effect.

'I thought you weren't all about looks,' she countered, and he visibly deflated with a sigh.

'I'm not,' he confessed, running his own hand through his hair, 'but lately it's got the better of me, just a bit.'

'Really?' she teased. 'So, what's changed?'

Memories of the photography session made her suddenly keen to see how the pictures had turned out. Now that she was with Carl again, nothing seemed quite the way that she had looked back on it — and he still had hold of her hand.

'I thought we were discussing you and your pictures,' he countered smoothly, his thumb rubbing the back of her hand, then it was gone as his hand dropped away.

Simon, the Deputy Editor, was staggering out of the downstairs loo and Jade felt an unhealthy resentment towards him for making Carl let go of her. The lounge door swung open as he went in and a wall of sound hit them. Jade could see the settee, chockablock with people lounging all over it, Brad and Mandy squashed up at one end. They appeared not the slightest bit bothered, even unaware of the partygoers crowded around them, and Jade wondered how they could hear themselves think, let alone hold a conversation, in noise like that.

A strange sensation flitted around her insides and, at first, it felt like a dose of jealousy, which would have seemed right but, as the door swung shut behind Simon, she realised with a jolt that she had no real fear of what might happen between them.

Surely that wasn't right? Even worse when she compared it with how she'd feel if Carl was kissing some other woman. The idea made her feel nauseous, but Carl wasn't hers and she had no right to him. Of course he could do what he wanted with anyone else. It was no business of hers.

'Are you ok?' Carl asked, as though reading her mind and she nodded, sensing how unconvincing she was by the quizzical look on his face. 'Have Mandy and Brad upset you?' he probed deep and she only just stopped herself from laughing at how wrong he'd got it.

'Maybe,' she lied, only ready to admit the truth to herself. She felt sort of free, for the first time in ages, not having to worry about whether Brad thought it was time to go home, or whether he was bored. This was the latest he'd been out for ages, barring his trip to Yorkshire, of course, and she had no idea what time he'd got in when he was away, but she'd set pretty good odds on the fact that he'd turned in before the netball team. Seeing him here at the party, she wondered if time existed for him now at all.

And here she was with Carl, with the opportunity to talk and no-one around particularly to listen but as she prepared to broach the subject which had erected a wall between them, his mobile rang in his trouser pocket. He drew it out quickly, looked at it for a long second, then glanced at Jade.

Apparently deciding better than to answer it, he shoved it back into his pocket, letting it cut into the answering machine whilst Jade's madness re-emerged. Who was this woman? Was it the same one as before? The jealousy that had evaded her a few moments earlier reared its dragon-like head and she failed to keep it under control.

'Carl, what the hell's going on with

you? Are you actually with someone else? One minute you're hot, then you go cold on me. You have other women ringing you and now you don't want to answer your phone 'cos I'm here.' It was all she could do not to poke him in the chest as she was ranting, with no thought for anyone who might come out into the hall. 'And don't deny it because I can see it in your eyes.'

All of a sudden the tempo changed in the lounge and the beat of a slow song seeped through the walls, but Jade's racing pulse wouldn't slow down along with it. She seethed with frustration and finally shoved Carl against the wall when he refused to answer her, but of course he was too strong for her. He eased her hands off with infuriating ease then shuffled her comically up the hall.

'I haven't got a woman,' he said plainly, his body up against hers as he pressed her against the wall. 'But I promise I will have before long.' The now so familiar brown eyes searched hers, challenging her to deny him, but she had no reply. 'And not just any woman, Jade. The woman for me. Does *Lady in Red* give you a clue?'

He looked up and she followed his gaze to a sprig of mistletoe hanging down from the lightshade above them. There was no doubt what would come next. She thought nothing could top the moment of feverish anticipation when his head lowered slowly to hers, the wait so exquisitely torturous, but when his lips brushed against hers, teasing as he withheld himself, she knew there was better to come.

The feather-light touch of his mouth against hers made every frazzled nerve cry out for him and she held herself back, equally determined not to crush his lips with her own. She wanted to taste him, feel the warmth of his lips.

Her heart sank as he moved his mouth away from her, working his way down her neck, near her cleavage, then back up to her throat. A shiver of pleasure quivered through her when he nipped at her earlobe and she savoured the fathomless ache beginning to spread low in her stomach.

She marvelled at the control he exerted, holding back from exploring her mouth, equal only to the control she was having to exercise in not begging for his kiss. Every cell in her body sought to mingle with his, but he continued to tantalise with the graze of his lips moving up her jaw and back to her mouth.

Her own lips parted in anticipation, wanting to draw him in, but instead he denied her for longer. She breathed his name, giving in, pleading with him to kiss her, but he just breathed her name back, forcing her to understand how much she wanted him. So that was it, she realised. That was what he wanted. His hunger for her was as great as hers was for him, but he was making her see the strength of it. Making her comprehend that they were fighting the tide.

Jade felt their bodies sway together to the rhythm of the music in the next room, even though she hadn't registered what the song was. They seemed to have somehow become one entity without any part of them locked together and his refusal to kiss her had made her feel heady. She leaned back against the wall, exhausted by his game and the thrill he sent through her each time his lips moved close to hers.

'I can't do this, Carl,' she breathed, but the tide suddenly turned in her favour and he consumed her with a kiss that made her lose all sense of grounding. Her body no longer felt hers as it seemed to seep into his.

'Jade?'

Jade slowly became aware that the music was louder. The lounge door had swung open and Mandy appeared in the hall, her blue eyes suddenly huge as she appeared to register that she had been right. When their gaze met, the inferno that Jade was engulfed in became swiftly doused into ash.

'Mandy . . . '

After staring for a moment, Mandy

turned and fled down the hall, leaving Jade smouldering in Carl's arms. Shattered, she leant against him, the heat of him making her dizzy and wishing the ground would swallow her up.

'She'll tell him,' she told Carl, bluntly. 'She's bound to tell him what she saw.' Her sigh was so deep she felt like a rag doll, empty of anything solid to keep her body erect.

'It's probably no worse than they've done. You saw them, Jade.' Carl drew away, his hand touching her head, stroking softly, trying to comfort, but Jade shook him off.

'I know him, Carl. He wouldn't. If Mandy fancies him, it'd take him a year to work it out.'

Carl's laugh filled the hall.

'If Mandy fancies him? Who are you kidding? You saw how she's been looking at him this evening. I've only seen her look at one bloke like that before.'

They both know that he meant

himself, but Jade said nothing and Carl's hand dropped to his side as he apparently sensed it wasn't having much of an effect. Jade was definitely not comforted and, after what was bound to now follow, she felt a sudden sadness that the friendship starting to blossom between her and Mandy would disappear before it had really even begun — and that was before she even considered what would happen between her and Brad.

Tears pricked at Jade's eyes and she brushed past Carl into the lounge to where she had left her clutchbag, tucked underneath an armchair. She trusted her colleagues, of course, but she had no idea who else lived in Kev's house. Having once had her bag pinched at a party, she'd become expert at keeping hers close or stashing it way out of sight.

Jade glanced at Brad, now standing up next to the speaker where she and Carl had been standing, but he was flicking through a plastic box of CDs, unaware of her presence, and she eased out of the room, grateful that she needn't say any goodbyes. She wanted to be gone before Mandy returned from the loo and created a scene.

'What . . . you're not leaving?' Carl said, waiting for her in the hall. 'Why don't you just stay here and face the music with me?'

Jade's hand was on the front door as she turned round to face him. 'Because, Carl, when it comes down to it, I still don't know what tune you're playing. I've probably just mucked up my life for no reason. You say you want me, you say you aren't seeing anyone else, but you never give any proper explanations. See you after Christmas, at work.'

The door shook in its frame behind her and for a split second she felt bad for the neighbours then heard the music blaring out of the house. It would make no difference in the scheme of things, and she strode down the road, grateful that, this time, it wasn't too far to her own place.

She was soon past Crofton Stores and down onto the duel carriageway then up Eastland Road.

When the key turned in the lock and she opened the door to the hall, she felt an incredible emptiness. The lack of Christmas paraphernalia suddenly made everything feel sad and totally meaningless. Not wishing to dwell on the barrenness of her lounge, she hurried upstairs and started the shower, desperate to wash the evening's events from her skin.

It was gone one o'clock when she slid gratefully under her duvet, thankful too that there was no need for the alarm the following morning. She sleepily placed her phone next to the bed and, within minutes, she was gone.

When the ringtone blared into the silence less than an hour later, she awoke with a start and the feeling that she had barely closed her eyes.

Jade looked at the display drowsily, but adrenalin forced her rudely awake when she saw Brad's name glowing in the darkness. For a moment she considered the idea of not answering but there was only so long that she could avoid him, so she picked up the mobile, her voice weak with guilt.

'Jade?'

Brad's voice, fresh and awake sounded peculiar in the early hours of the morning, as if it belonged to another world.

'I didn't want to freak you out by ringing the doorbell but I'm standing outside,' he continued, not waiting for a response. 'Can I come in?'

15

The pounding of her pulse buzzed in Jade's ears. Brad was outside? She knew she had no real choice but to let him in now that he knew she was awake, but the thought of the inevitable confrontation after what Mandy saw in Kev's hall filled her with dread. A sudden thought escalated her stress as she told Brad she'd be down in a minute. What if he'd brought Mandy along, to back up his claim?

Slipping her arms into her dressing gown and her feet into her fluffy pink slipper boots, she felt at even more of a disadvantage as she trudged down the stairs. Somehow, being in nightclothes put one at a psychological disadvantage and she wished she was still dressed up to the nines; then reality seeped through in an instant. It didn't matter what she was wearing or how much she was done up, the truth was the truth and there was no way to evade it.

She unbolted the front door and opened it to the night and a slightly bedraggled Brad on the doorstep. It had started to drizzle since she'd got home.

'Come in, Brad.' Jade peered subtly outside the door for Brad's companion but he was alone. 'Do you want a hot drink?'

'A hot chocolate would be good. I doubt you've got decaf coffee?'

Jade shook her head and led the way through to the kitchen, filled the kettle and switched it on. When she turned round, Brad was already seated at the kitchen table, damp jacket draped over the back of the chair.

'You left without saying goodbye.'

The statement hung in the air, veering more towards being a question and Jade sensed a tripwire, ready for her to set off. He looked slightly forlorn with his chin in his hands, peering up at her, and Jade's heart missed a beat. She wanted to take him in her arms and make it all better. She wished she could wipe out all she'd done wrong.

How could she have hurt such a simple, unpretentious man as Brad was?

'I'm sorry, Brad,' she said uneasily, willing the kettle to boil. 'I was just so tired and you were otherwise occupied, so I came on home. It wasn't far to walk.'

Brad's sigh seemed to hit every wall before it reached its target and Jade wished she could have ducked. It was hauled from his heart, heavy as a hammer, with the potential to strike a mortal blow.

Silence roosted between them as each appeared to struggle for what to say next, then the click of the kettle sliced through it and Jade busied herself thankfully with spoonfuls of hot chocolate and lashings of aerosol cream for herself. Finally, there was no escape from the need to sit down and she passed Brad's drink across the table, sipping gingerly at her own.

He caught her eye and the next thing out of his mouth almost took her breath away.

'I'm sorry, Jade. I really am. I

completely ignored you tonight and spent most of the evening with Mandy. I'm assuming you saw us slow-dancing and that's why you left?'

His finger traced a ring around the rim of the cup and his blond fringe had dropped down over one eye, reminding Jade of how vulnerable he could look. The turquoise of his eyes was piercing, even at this hour when he'd normally have been asleep. She sat back, almost winded by Brad's admission and how he had just turned the tables on himself.

'I didn't see you slow-dancing, Brad. I didn't know that you did. I just saw you talking with Mandy all night. You seem to have been getting on well so I thought I would leave you to it.' Her finger gathered a smattering of cream and she licked it from her fingertip. 'It's not the end of the world.'

As Jade said it, she wasn't sure that was the case. In one evening, she had kissed Carl, and Brad had danced with and spent hours talking to an office colleague. Perhaps it wasn't the end of the world, but it might be the end of things as they were.

'No, but it still wasn't right,' Brad said, sharply. 'I shouldn't have been dancing with Mandy. I should have been dancing with you. You're my girlfriend, Jade, and I'm sorry.'

So, here it was now, Jade realised . . . the precise time for her to apologise and clear the air with Brad. There was no point in him saving it up to attack her with it later. Her fingers gripped her cup as she forced the difficult words out of her mouth.

'And I shouldn't have been kissing Carl, Brad. That wasn't right either. I'm sorry too. Perhaps we can just — '

'What?'

In the shortest of moments, Brad no longer looked vulnerable as his head jerked up and his turquoise eyes darkened to a storm. Jade recoiled from his threatening stare.

'M-Mandy must have told you?' she stammered, fear and surprise flushing through her simultaneously. The split second realisation that Mandy had kept her sordid secret somehow made her feel worse. The kitchen seemed suddenly tiny as Brad's stature grew, the scrape of his chair making her teeth clench as he pushed it away.

'No, she didn't tell me! Do you think I'd be sitting here apologising if she had?'

Jade could do nothing but shake her head, unable to dredge up a response. Her hands gripped the cup harder as she tried to draw out enough heat to counter the chill in her body.

'You kissed him?' he went on, running his hand through his hair as though in disbelief. 'You kissed Carl?' He threw his hands up, scaring her with his vehemence. 'Don't you think I wanted to kiss Mandy? But I didn't 'cos I'm in a relationship with you.'

Stunned by his declaration, Jade stared at the grooves in the table, letting his words sink in but wishing they wouldn't.

The strength of Brad and Mandy's connection had been no product of her imagination. Brad had wanted Mandy, in the same way that she'd wanted Carl. How long, she wondered, had Brad felt that way? Was it before tonight?

'So you danced with her. Romantic dancing. Close up. Body to body.' Jade stated the fact.

'But I didn't kiss her!' Brad's indignation had him pacing the floor and the stress of his anger made Jade want to flee the room, but at the same time she wanted to understand where this was going.

'But you wanted to,' she said calmly. 'What does that say?'

Brad looked at her, anger and confusion creasing his tanned forehead. 'Well, it says that I had more restraint than you. It says that I at least have some principles. It says that I — '

'Probably should leave and we'll talk about this tomorrow.' Jade raised her voice above Brad's, no longer cowed by his anger but fed up with his holier than thou attitude. 'Look, I've said I'm sorry, Brad, and there's nothing we can do about all this tonight. We both need some sleep. Do you need a settee to sleep on? You can stay here if you want.'

She thought it was unfair to kick him out now after he had come over, but Brad looked as if she had lost her mind.

Brad shook his head sadly. 'So that's what we've come to? You upstairs and me on the settee?'

Now it was Jade's turn to look baffled. She'd thought his expression of horror was shock that she'd even offered. The thought of sharing her bed in this sort of mood made her wince.

'Brad, for goodness sake. Neither of us will get any sleep. Do you want the settee or not?'

Now she was standing, cup in hand, feeling much more in control. For a moment, she wondered if the neighbours had heard their yelling, but Brad's reply interrupted her thoughts.

'No thanks, Jade. I'd rather be in my own bed. If that's how you feel, I'll see you tomorrow. Are you still coming over?'

Jade sighed, still confused at the turn

of the conversation. Brad's anger seemed to have dissipated fast and in its place was a sort of righteous indignation. She even began to wonder if he'd actually been jealous at all.

'Do you still want this?' she asked, offering him his hot chocolate. He took it from her, his hand still slightly clammy and damp from the drizzle outside, drinking it down in large gulps as she tipped the rest of hers down the sink. 'I'll come after dinner,' she told him. 'I'll be over at Mum and Dan's before that. Although you're welcome to join us, of course,' she added, with a sardonic smile.

She watched as Brad swished his cup under the tap then brazenly declared that his car was in need of a good going over. 'After dinner then,' Jade confirmed, seeing him to the door.

The rain had worsened since Brad's arrival and her gaze followed him as he made his way up the street, probably headed into town to grab a taxi back home.

Grateful that she wasn't out in it herself, she trudged back upstairs and flopped into bed in the hope of returning to sleep but, of course, there wasn't a chance.

The minutes ticked on as she relentlessly turned the evening over in her mind, then her and Brad's subsequent argument. There was a sort of inevitability about the evening that she wished she'd been sensible enough to avoid, but nevertheless it was a strange-looking jigsaw and something, somewhere, didn't quite fit.

As she lay there, once more counting back from a thousand, that something niggled continually at the back of her mind, which she couldn't quite grasp. It was what Brad had said when admitting his feelings for Mandy; something about why he had refused to go with the flow of his lust. And then Jade remembered his words . . .

But I didn't 'cos I'm in a relationship with you.

Brad hadn't said it was because he

had loved her, or because she was the girl that he wanted to marry. He hadn't kissed a woman he'd wanted to be with because he was 'in a relationship' with Jade.

This thought didn't help her to drift off into oblivion. Instead, Jade lay awake until dawn, when she finally slept from exhaustion.

* * *

Christmas Eve properly broke for her at just after ten in the form of a crisp, sunny morning and an insistent ring at the front door. Reluctantly, she pulled on her dressing gown yet again, tripping over her shoes as she rushed downstairs to answer it and hoping it wasn't Brad returning for round two.

As she approached the front door, she could see through the frosted panel there was no need to panic, she was safe. The red postman's overcoat put her at ease and she accepted the parcel from him with thanks. Nevertheless, the flat, rectangular package could mean only one thing and Jade unwrapped it with trepidation, knowing that she couldn't put off looking at the photos from Carl any longer. This was the last present that needed wrapping and she needed to do it before she went out.

Jade went straight to her workbag, determined to get it done as soon as possible, then she could properly start the day. The envelope was unsealed and she drew the photos out and placed them on the kitchen table, having made sure it was clean first. The CD was there too and she breathed a sigh of relief that she wouldn't yet have to face the more intimate pictures. When she was ready, she could do that in her own time.

The A4 sized photo on top was in black and white, then another, identical but in colour, underneath. Carl had given her a choice for each photo, she realised, flicking through the ones on the top. There were six photos of Jade in Carl's photography studio and she had to admit that, although she quite liked all of them, Carl had been right about the photo of her looking to the side. Dan would love it and she looked wonderfully natural. In fact, she looked more at ease than she had ever imagined in a posed photo and she became intrigued as to how she'd looked in the ones Carl had taken of her in his lounge.

At last, after she'd clipped her chosen picture into the new frame for Dan and wrapped it with a sheet of black shiny paper dotted with reindeers, curiosity got the better of her and, with nervous thoughts of what that had done to the cat, she drew the CD out of the envelope and took it upstairs.

Before long, it was whirring in her laptop and she clicked on 'Computer', then 'Drive D'. The photos came up as thumbnails and she timidly clicked on each one to expand them on the screen, at first hardly daring to look. Every image took her back to the evening at Carl's and how she had felt during their session, but instead of the shame she'd been expecting, she was filled with a kind of euphoria. She could almost hear the continuous click of the shutter. Flicking through each image now, there was nothing sordid, as she had feared; just pictures of a young woman.

At first she was fully clothed, then her blouse buttons were open. When she reached the photos of her in her bra, they looked every bit as professional as the ones Carl had up on his studio wall. He had done his job well, guiding her movements, putting Jade at ease and now, having seen them, she was quite disappointed that Carl hadn't printed these off as well. But she certainly wasn't going to ask him. No matter what chemistry there was between them, it had come to a close and she wouldn't relight the touch-paper again.

She forced back the memories of him as he worked and the touch of his hands on her back, refusing to give in to the way that they still made her feel.

She had bridges to mend with Brad and she couldn't do that with half her mind on somebody else. Returning the CD to its sleeve, she turned off the laptop, put it back under the bed and determined to get on with her day.

First stop was a long, scented, bubbly bath before driving over to Linda and Dan's just after midday. She'd decided to surprise them with one of Dan's favourite treats, after ringing to check that they weren't up to anything much already, and Jade knew the outing wouldn't harm her either, distracting her mind from recent events. Both Dan and Linda loved action movies and Jade booked tickets before they left for the new Bond film on her phone, to ensure they wouldn't miss out.

Armed with popcorn and coke, Jade dumped Dan's healthy eating plan with impressive abandon, and Dan sat through the whole film without a murmur, his attention never wavering from the screen except for a loo break.

Two-and-three-quarter hours later

they emerged into the darkening afternoon. The car park was starting to empty of last minute buyers as the shops began to close and Jade was relieved that she had been organised so far in advance.

'What time tomorrow?' Linda asked, as Jade helped Dan back into the house. She had perked up considerably compared to how she had been over recent weeks and Jade felt hopeful that she might be on the up. Christmas had always been Linda's down time, so for her to be so much better on Christmas Eve of all days was a positive sign.

'About ten ok with you?'

Jade kissed Dan on top of his head, which he rubbed off in mock disgust. Then, appearing to have second thoughts, he threw his arms around her, although drawing the line at kissing her back.

'Thanks, Jade. That was awesome!'

The smile on her brother's face was all the Christmas present Jade needed and, when she looked at Linda bustling around the tree, she began to realise that some things you could hold onto for far too long. She had been so much more selfish than Linda, who had always endeavoured to make the house look festive for Dan. Next year, Jade resolved, she would decorate every room in her house. Well, perhaps not every room, she smiled to herself, but the lounge, at least.

'Jade? I said ten o'clock's fine.'

Jade looked up as her mother flopped onto the settee. The afternoon had taken it out of her, but she was making so much effort it was a weight off Jade's shoulders to see her like this.

'Right. Great . . . well, see you then,' she said, taking her leave to grab a bite before heading off to Brad's place.

For the first time in a long while she felt a buzz of excitement in her stomach at the prospect of Christmas Day. She knew Dan would be thrilled with his iPad and it would be great to all eat Christmas dinner together, as well as the perfect chance for Brad to bond with Dan for a bit.

16

Desperate times called for desperate measures, Jade thought, as she scraped the last of the milk out of her cereal bowl. Brad must have been thinking something when he had sent her the gift at the office. He surely must still fancy her or he wouldn't have bothered buying lingerie.

Perhaps, she thought, this was all her fault anyway. Maybe he was put out that she hadn't worn it with him yet? Was that why there'd been little between them, of late? Then she remembered the night before Brad had gone to Yorkshire and how she had offered to wear it then, but she dismissed the memory before it settled too firmly in her mind. He would have been stressed out about the trip and whether he'd packed all he needed, and she was sure that he'd been exhausted after their run.

In the bedroom, Jade stripped off and put on the new underwear, taking her time doing up the ties of the panties into neat little bows. It could have been made for her and she twisted and turned in front of the mirror, feeling warm at the thought of Brad thinking of her when he chose it. The idea of him thinking of Mandy whilst he was deciding fleetingly stole into her mind, but she pushed it back out straight away, cross with herself for spoiling the moment. The lingerie fitted her to perfection and there was no way he had been thinking of anyone else.

Flicking through clothes in the wardrobe, she chose a pencil skirt she knew Brad was keen on, and a top that matched the emerald green of her eyes. The brown eye make-up she used made her think of Mandy the previous night, but again she pushed the memory away, determined to ensure that this evening would be a new start for her and Brad. They had both made mistakes, she could see that, but their relationship was far from beyond salvation.

She applied her mascara with generous strokes, emphasising her already long lashes, and chose a deep red liner for her lips. The scarlet lipstick that she knew Brad liked accentuated her full lips, and foundation, powder and blusher followed, on her cheeks. Her pearl hairclip completed the look and she stood back, knowing she looked fit to kill. Brad would love it, for sure.

She looked at his present peeking out, wrapped and ready, near the top of a bag filled with presents for Dan and Linda, but there was no point in taking it for him this evening. She wasn't one for opening presents early and she'd give it to him tomorrow so that he couldn't be tempted to cheat.

She had found a beautiful gold and onyx eagle signet ring in a jewellers in town that she knew he would adore and, although it had been a bit over her intended budget, she hadn't been able to resist. Once wrapped, it had looked a bit pathetic and somewhat obvious what it was, so she'd resorted to the age-old trick of placing it in a slightly larger box.

At seven, she pulled on her long red, woollen coat and at ten past she drew up outside Brad's, the heater in her car having barely kicked in. The temperature had dropped dramatically and Jade was glad of the gloves she'd warmed on the radiator before leaving the house.

Brad answered the doorbell almost as soon as she had pressed it and, seeing him dressed up to the nines in a pale pink shirt and dark jacket, she'd forgotten how handsomely chic he could look.

'Erm, am I forgetting something?' she asked, stepping inside. Surely they'd planned an evening in?

Brad hesitated, hands in his trouser pockets.

'Some of the others last night invited us down the pub,' he explained. 'Said they'd be there from about seven so I thought we could go for a bit?'

'Right.'

Jade's antennae were up, immediately suspicious as to his motives. Would Mandy Jones be there? she wondered, considering the idea of refusing to go; but then she'd never know what he'd had planned if she didn't. She was certainly dressed up enough to go out and she guessed that the lingerie could wait until later.

'Sounds like a good idea,' she replied, with as much enthusiasm as she could muster. 'You want to go now?'

'Might as well.' Brad collected his keys from the table.

'I'll drive, Brad. I don't want to drink anyway. I've had more than enough lately.'

Brad's response was a shrug, his arm slipping around her as he closed the front door behind them and they faced the chill of a bitter Christmas Eve.

At least now the heater was prepped and ready to go, and Jade's feet enjoyed the blast of it defrosting her toes. They were too soon back in town. Parked by the church in the centre, they walked to the pub, inevitably finding it heaving.

A couple of friends had got themselves chicken and chips in a basket. Others were standing around with their drinks. Jade's gaze was as sharp as a switchblade and she looked around, searching anxiously for either Mandy or Carl, but neither were to be seen.

A sense of calm flooded through her and she considered that perhaps Brad's appetite for socialising had been whetted by his nights away and the previous night out. Maybe he was beginning to loosen up a bit and the pair of them could have a bit more fun. Remembering that some very sexy underwear lingered beneath her sophisticated outerwear, Jade felt quite loosened up herself. She ordered a diet cola and asked Brad what he would like, but he insisted he wanted the same.

'I'm driving, remember?' Jade said, but Brad was resolute.

'I'm still suffering a bit from last night.'

He glanced away from her towards

the door and Jade followed his gaze, but there was no-one there for him to look at.

She ordered the drinks and together they joined a small group near the bar. Simon was regaling them all with stories of his days on a national paper in London. Love had dragged him away from the City to the green fields of Somerset; it hadn't worked out but he'd found his feet at the Observer, gained Deputy Editor, and fallen in love with the town.

As Simon talked, Jade slipped her hand into Brad's and he looked at her and smiled briefly, making her feel like a child and slightly perplexed as to why he was so happy to be with the crowd. It was unlike him, as he usually hung back in the shadows unless he was organising the show. There was no inbetween with Brad Wilson, but today he was definitely acting out of character.

Undeterred, Jade waited until some of the people dispersed and then whispered loudly in his ear, above the hum of conversation, 'I can't wait until later,' she told him. 'I'm wearing your present. Thought you might like to see.'

Immediately, Brad's gaze dropped to her hands then back up to her face. 'The nail varnish and make-up?'

His blue eyes revealed his puzzlement. Jade looked down. She had no nail varnish on.

'No. Did you buy that as well?'

She should have guessed, she realised; the make-up was perfect for her eyes and the nail varnish definitely wasn't cheap. Silently, she cursed herself for not remembering to put the nail varnish on, but there seemed to be more than that to worry about when she next caught Brad's gaze. It almost scorched her and she took a mental step back, her hand dropping to her side.

'As well? D'you mean as well as that underwear?'

His voice had risen in volume and she looked around, concerned that someone might be listening. Airing her dirty linen in public really wasn't her scene. Jade knew she must look completely perplexed as Brad continued to practically shout at her. 'It wasn't my gift. It was probably from Army Boy. He's certainly weird enough to buy something like that.'

This time, Jade took a real step back, shocked by Brad's sudden vehemence. Army boy? What was he on about? Had he flipped his mind? Brad hadn't really put anything behind him when it came to last night at all. It was all there, bubbling under the surface, ready to submerge Jade in its depths.

'What do you mean 'weird'?' she said, quietly. Although she had no right to be, she felt hotly protective of Carl's reputation, at the same time aware that it was a bad idea to let it show.

Brad thumped his empty glass down on the bar.

'Well, he's all messed up, isn't he? I'm sure you know all about it. Serves him right, if you ask me. He was probably fooling about where he shouldn't be. In the wrong place, with the wrong person. Like last night.'

Apparently delighted with his comparison, Brad leant back on a bar stool, as if challenging her to respond, but Jade was stunned into silence.

Army? she kept asking herself. How could she not have known something like that? She felt such a fool.

'Since you seem to know everything,' she challenged back. 'Please do go on . . . '

'He got himself blown up on tour. Trashed his back, apparently, but I'm sure you've seen it. No wonder he didn't join in the Full Monty . . . '

'At least he had a good reason!' Jade interrupted hotly, her understanding growing with each of Brad's words. 'So, what was yours, then? I'm surprised you even noticed what Carl was doing, you were so engrossed in your 'conversation' with someone else.'

As Jade spoke, the past slipped into the present, beginning to make sense

. . . how Carl hadn't wanted to take his shirt off; how there were no remnants of his past around his flat. She could only assume that he wanted to put his army days behind him and try to move on, but it didn't seem to be working and it was all so confused, with his celebratory photos of people with disabilities alongside his apparent inability to accept his own.

Then there were the phone calls. There was so much about him that she just didn't know or understand. While part of her wanted to run to him and help him see that she adored him regardless, a greater part screamed at her it was far wiser to keep clear.

'No thanks, mate,' Brad was saying, and Jade realised that Terry was asking if they'd like a drink.

She smiled politely, shaking her head, feeling almost shell-shocked. Subconsciously, she had confessed how much she thought of Carl Heaney, and her conscious mind was now doing little to rebuff the idea. Instead, it allowed the admission to circulate, battering all other thoughts into submission, but she refused to give in. She wished she could wipe Carl out of her mind. There was still tomorrow to contend with and Dan was expecting to spend it with Linda, Jade and Brad. She would never do anything to ruin Dan's special day.

Brad's stilted conversation with Terry was awkward to hear and Jade was relieved when Terry finally picked up the vibes and moved on.

'Well, tomorrow's going to be fun, isn't it?' she said to Brad sarcastically, picking up the thread. 'I came out tonight thinking we could start afresh and make a proper go of things. We need to be adult about this, Brad. Put aside our differences for Dan's sake, at least.'

Brad's blue eyes avoided hers yet again and this time she sensed that something big was amiss.

'Brad?' she prompted. 'I said we need to be grown-ups and make tomorrow work. There's nothing either of us has done that we can't work out.'

'I won't be here tomorrow,' Brad said, flatly. 'I'm driving to Bristol at around nine thirty tonight. I'm booked into a Travelodge.'

'With Mandy?'

Brad met her gaze, looking almost amused.

'No, not Mandy! Mum and Dad are driving down right now and they've booked us a table in town. They wanted us to spend the day together and as I rarely see them . . . '

His voice trailed off and Jade thought that at least he had the decency to feel a little bit bad. She looked at the empty glass on the bar.

'So that's why you're not drinking. Crikey, Brad. You're more full of surprises than I expected. Well, go and enjoy yourself with your parents, and say hello from me because I know how much they like me, and my brother who's so unwell.'

Brad blinked hard, as if he'd been slapped. 'What? What are you on about, Jade?' But she knew that he knew, from the sheepishness in his voice.

'I'm not stupid, Brad. They just want perfection for their only son and there's a good chance that I'm not it. They know Dan's illness is genetic and I may be a carrier. Your dad's a GP, for heaven's sake!'

The truth that had laid unspoken between them for so long them crept out of her Pandora's box, killing the conversation dead. There was no contradiction, no disagreement, no defiant denial of Jade's way of thinking, but she pushed Brad some more.

'You couldn't face Christmas Day with Dan, could you?' she confronted him, her hand almost breaking the glass she still held. 'Could you?' she almost screamed.

Brad's voice dropped almost to an undertone. 'He's unpredictable. You've got to admit that. People stare and I don't want my Christmas Day ruined.'

'Huh?' She paused for a moment, astounded. 'You're serious, aren't you? You really are obsessed with perfection.

You're as bad as your parents. Your fitness, your homemade food, the way you look, how you like me to dress. Life is life, Brad. It's not something we keep in a box to keep it flawless. We're all broken . . . just some more than others.' She paused again, looking at him for a long moment. 'In some of us, it just doesn't show.'

She dumped her glass angrily onto the counter and stormed out of the pub, leaving Brad adrift at the bar. She barely noticed the temperature drop outside and nor, it appeared, did others as they wandered in the street in dresses and T-shirts without coats. Striding towards the car park, Jade was warmed by the bubble of satisfaction that came with leaving Brad in the lurch, but it was Christmas Eve and she knew he had no transport to get home. Cursing aloud and finally turning around, she gave it five or so more minutes, then returned to the pub where Brad was still alone, propping the bar up, deep in thought.

'Well, come on, then, if you want to get home,' she spat at him, angrily.

She made him trail in her wake all the way back to the car park, the sharp and rapid click of her heels on the pavement echoing into the night, along with the shouts of a few revellers in town. A few hours later and St John's church would be full for midnight mass.

'Get in the car, Brad,' Jade said finally, opening the doors with the remote. 'I don't really know why I'm bothering. I ought to make you pay for a taxi but take this as your Christmas present.' She sighed, giving him a long, lingering look as she recognised the significance of the moment. 'It's the last you'll ever get from me.'

17

The colourful lights and shop decorations in town now made her house seem plainer as each day passed. Jade tossed her keys onto the beanbag, throwing herself onto the settee. She was exhausted to the bone. She had seen enough of the road between Yeovil and Sherborne to last her a lifetime and was more than happy not to be on it again for some time. *Too many memories*, she thought despondently, convinced that Brad Wilson was now just a memory, although she'd still have to face him at work.

To have banged out on her like that after eighteen months of their relationship was unreal. She wished he'd had the courage to face his feelings a lot earlier, but now she had seen his true colours and assumed they had been affected in no small part by his parents.

It hurt, and she knew Dan would be

confused when only Jade turned up tomorrow but, in truth, she would have a more relaxed Christmas Day without having to worry about Brad as well.

Jade flicked on the TV and scrolled through the guide, finding most of the decent stuff was already halfway through. After trying eight or nine channels, she settled on *It's a Wonderful Life*, an apparent Christmas classic that she had never bothered with before. It was close to the end and it soon turned on Jade's waterworks, and twenty minutes in, the emotions broke through like a dam-burst and Jade knew that Christmas could never become a time she could love.

How could history repeat itself so cruelly? She thought back to the distressing sounds of her father leaving on that Christmas Eve, and how Brad had effectively done the same to her now. That morning, she had harboured a determination to give their relation-ship all that she had, but there was no going back from tonight. At some time, she would have to pick up the belongings she'd left at Brad's flat, but there was nothing she was in need of. In reality, she could avoid Brad Wilson for as long as she wished: their paths shouldn't cross too often professionally other than being in the same office. Jade was sure she could move desks to further away if she spoke to Jenny in confidence.

Brad Wilson . . . great writer; dashing good looks; fit, athletic body. Jade knew he was any woman's fantasy. She just couldn't believe how shallow he'd turned out to be.

Forcing herself off the settee, she went into the kitchen to grab a tissue and heard the unmistakeable tone of a text coming through on her phone. Suddenly immobile, her first instinct was to leave it where it was — there was no way she wanted any exchange with Brad, no matter the medium. She just wanted to be left alone to lick her wounds in peace.

Tomorrow she would have to make an astronomical effort to convince

Linda and Dan that all was well and she was ok with Brad not being there, but for now there was no need for her to keep up pretences.

An unopened bottle of Baileys, which had sat in the cupboard since her birthday in August, was calling quite insistently, and she took a small glass from the cupboard above the kettle and dropped in a couple of ice cubes.

Why the hell not? she thought, glugging some into the glass, then settling back down in front of the TV. There was no harm in having a little. She deserved it after the evening she'd had, and she would start her teetotal regime again after Christmas Day. She tried to forget that this time it had only lasted a few hours.

The film was coming to a close and her mind flicked back to Linda and Dan, then to the text that had come through. What if it had been from her mum? Dan might be over excited and being a bit of a handful. Perhaps Linda needed some help?

Jade pulled out her phone from her bag and unlocked it to discover a text from an unknown number. Once it was open, she couldn't resist the temptation to read.

Hi Jade. I've had a text from Brad saying he's going to Bristol for Xmas. Didn't sound like u were with him. I hope nothing happened after last night. I'd hate to b the cause of anything awful. I didn't tell him what I saw. Please text back. Mandy.

Jade sat back, the screen bright in the semi-darkness, her mind in a spin. Mandy was the last person she'd have expected to hear from — it would have been easier for her to keep her head low, but it appeared she'd chosen to poke her head above the parapet and contact Jade herself.

Jade re-read the words, then read them again more slowly, to digest them, uncertain whether it was a good thing or bad that Mandy Jones wasn't yet a really close friend. She could easily have told Brad what she'd seen between Jade and Carl at the party and Jade certainly had that to thank her for, even though she had now confessed it herself.

But what was Brad doing with Mandy's number? Had they been exchanging texts before tonight?

Her phone now on standby, Jade unlocked it again and begun to text back. *Can we talk?* she responded briefly.

Then she began polishing off her Baileys, waiting to see if the phone would ring after all.

She didn't have to wait long. A layer of beige creamy liquid clung to the top half of her glass as her ringtone drowned out James Stewart's unmistakeable voice.

Jade stared at it for a few moments, uncertain now as to whether she had made the right decision to speak to Mandy, but just as the answering service was about to kick in, she pressed the green button.

'Hello?'

'Jade?'

'Yes, it's Jade.'

A short silence divided them as well

as the distance between their homes, if that was in fact where Mandy was ringing from. Then Mandy spoke again.

'I wanted to make sure you were alright. When Brad texted, it sounded a bit of a mess. To be honest, Jade, I don't really get quite what's going on. I didn't know things weren't right with you two, but last night . . . '

'You're not with Brad now, are you, Mandy?' Jade interrupted, suspicious of Mandy's motives. She muted the TV to see if she could hear anything in the background, but there was nothing.

'Of course I'm not with him!' Mandy responded tartly, and Jade felt reassured by her terseness. It was good to see she had backbone after all. 'Why would I be ringing you if I was?'

Jade couldn't find a sensible answer so remained silent, waiting for Mandy to go on.

'The truth is, I was worried I'd messed things up, talking with Brad so much yesterday evening. It was out of order, looking back, but we seemed to have so much to chat about, I don't think either of us realised how it must have looked. When you'd left without saying goodbye, I thought . . . '

'You weren't just talking though, were you, Mandy? Brad said there was some dancing involved.'

Now it was Mandy's turn to go silent and Jade waited to see how Mandy could squirm out of this situation, but was surprised to find that she didn't at all.

'There was one dance, you're right, and yes, it was a slow dance, but we didn't kiss, Jade. Nothing like that.'

'But you wanted to?' Jade needed to know, wanted to be prepared for what she might have to face in the office now that her and Brad's relationship was over. 'I know for a fact that Brad wanted to kiss you.'

'He did?' Mandy's tone rose, telegraphing her astonishment. 'How d'you know that?'

Jade sipped at the cool liquid that warmed her as it went down her throat, feeling oddly calm.

'He told me,' she said. 'Last night, when I told him that I'd kissed Carl.'

'You told him? Why would you do that?'

Mandy's veneer was beginning to crack and her voice became shrill, as it did when she got over excited, and Jade preferred it when she was a little less ruffled. She felt it wise to try and restore Mandy's composure so that the conversation could resume as usefully as possible.

'We're way past that mattering, Mandy. He isn't able to accept my family and that affects our potential future. I guess I've known that for some time, but I just didn't want to admit to myself that it wasn't really working.'

'And you have feelings for Carl?'

'I guess that's obvious.'

'It certainly looked that way when I saw you last night.' Mandy gave a tentative laugh. 'Well, it's looked that way for quite a long time. Everyone in the office thinks there's something going on with

you both. To tell you the truth, Jade . . . '
Mandy paused, gathering her courage,
Jade supposed, ' . . . nobody really gets
why you're with Brad.'

In the solitude of her house, with
only a mute TV for company, Jade felt
the heat of a blush on her cheeks at the
thought of her feelings being so obvious, mortified at the idea of the office
staff talking about her.

Agitated by the turn of the conversation, she went into the kitchen and turned
on the kettle for no real reason other
than a distraction. She left the room as
the vibrations of the kettle made it impossible to hear on the phone.

'Well, it doesn't matter too much
what I think of him,' she said bluntly,
aware that Mandy had been waiting for
her response. 'I'm not getting involved
with anyone at the moment, and
certainly not someone like Carl.'

In all the to-do with Brad, Jade had
forgotten Mandy's longtime obsession
for Carl and was badly prepared for her
vehement riposte.

'That's a bit rich, Jade, when you've been flirting with him for ages. What d'you mean 'someone like Carl'? I thought you really liked him.'

The accusation took Jade aback and she withdrew from the phone, quietly considering what Mandy had said. It was true, of course; she had been blatantly flirting with him, and he with her, and she'd been attracted to him for a long time, but she also knew that she couldn't share him. If he had someone else, then there was no way she would get involved.

Should she tell Mandy? How much could she trust her when she probably still had a thing for Carl Heaney, although Mandy did appear now to rather like Brad as well?

Who else could she talk to, though? Jade decided to bite the bullet. Other than Mandy, she was pretty much on her own. She didn't fancy confiding in her mother — there was so much to explain and Linda had enough in her own life to think about.

'I reckon Carl already has a girl-friend,' Jade told Mandy, then waited for her response.

'What?' Mandy laughed aloud. 'No-one from the office has ever seen him out with a woman. Believe me, I'd be the first person they'd tell if they had. Some of them in that place love winding me up.'

Jade knew that much was true, at least, and it didn't make her feel comfortable. People could be cruel and more than once she had tried to dissuade Kev from annoying Mandy in the past.

So, perhaps it was a distance relationship? Jade reasoned, if no-one had seen him out and about with a female; but then, she had heard Carl mention calling round during the phone call she'd overheard. It had sounded like someone living nearby.

The credits rolled at the end of the film, and Jade left the TV on as a source of light. In the room, the flickering shadows lessened as the screen darkened, reflecting Jade's mood.

'I don't know, Mandy. I'm so confused,'

Jade confessed, at last, wishing she could just close her eyes and pretend that none of this was happening.

She knew that kissing Carl was a symptom for things not working with Brad, and if she had never gone for that portrait, maybe things would never have kicked off. If she told herself that often enough, Jade thought wryly, she might even begin to believe it.

'You never answered, Mandy,' she pressed, attempting to switch the tables. 'How do you feel about Brad?'

Mandy appeared to be thinking and Jade could hear her breathing through the phone. When she did eventually answer, her tone would have given her feelings away whatever she said.

'I don't think I realised until last night,' she began slowly, 'what he was really like. I have to admit, although I still fancy Carl, Brad is more my type of guy. He's simple and straightforward, not like Carl who's quite an enigma. I realised that the day he came with me to do the photos.'

Mandy caught her breath and paused as if deciding whether or not to go on.

'Honestly? I think perhaps Carl has been a bit of a schoolgirl crush, whereas Brad . . . well, I could see the difference. We had so much in common. I know it might sound boring but we were talking about health policies for hours at the party. I probably shouldn't say all this when you and Brad . . . well . . . ' Her voice trailed off.

Jade groaned aloud, with an accompanying laugh.

'Sounds like you two are made for each other,' she said, sadness tainting her voice. 'I know that stuff about policies is important but there's only so much of it I can take!'

A regret settled deep in her stomach, that she couldn't have been more what Brad needed, and Brad more what she needed.

'So, what about Carl?' It was Mandy's turn to press the point home. 'You're not telling me that you're just going to ignore what's happened?

Surely it needs to be resolved one way or the other? Why don't you just ask him if he has somebody else?'

'I did.'

'And?'

'Obviously he denied it.'

'So why do you think he has, then?'

'I heard him on the phone to a woman when I was there. It sounded intimate.' Jade sighed, remembering how he had called the woman 'beautiful' and offered to call round.

'Hmm.'

'What?' Jade was aware how the dialogue had changed from two women on their guard to a sort of female collusion and she liked the sense of being supported by what was starting to feel like a friend.

'Well, it's just that I've heard him on the phone a few times in the office and it patently wasn't to do with work. Once I heard him setting times for a meeting . . . crikey . . . must have been over a year ago now. Could it have been something like that?'

'Hmm.' Jade's response echoed Mandy's as she mulled the idea over. 'I don't know — it just sounded too personal . . .'

'Go over and ask him! What else are you going to do on Christmas Eve? Sit there and stew?'

Jade blinked as the screen brightened again at the end of the credits and an advert for *The Muppet Christmas Carol* blazed colourfully into the room. Outside, an ambulance siren blared its way to or from the nearby hospital.

Should she go over? She looked at the half empty glass of Baileys. It was tiny; she'd never be over the limit after that.

'How will you feel tomorrow, on Christmas Day? If you don't do it now, when will you?'

'I just don't think men and Christmas mix. For me, it's not been a good combination . . .'

'Then it's time to break the mould. I've seen how you look at each other, for goodness sake. Go get your coat!'

Jade laughed aloud at how the tables

had turned from their office relationship. At work it had always been Jade setting Mandy straight or reassuring her; now, Mandy was returning the compliment in a manner that Jade had never expected. She could be good for Brad, she realised. They had a lot in common, of course, but Mandy also appeared to have the understanding that someone like Brad needed.

'Ok, you win!' she said, at last. 'I'm turning the TV off and getting my coat. Happy?'

'Good. You need to know one way or another.'

'So, what are you doing tomorrow?' Jade suddenly realised she had no idea of Mandy Jones' plans.

'Oh, not a lot. I'm driving up to my parents in Suffolk on the 28th for a late Christmas celebration. They're on a cruise 'til the 27th. Lucky them!'

The matchmaking side of Jade kick-started her thoughts. 'You could always pop up to Bristol. I'm sure Brad's parents would love to meet you and the restaurant is sure to be able to squeeze in one more.'

As the words came out of her mouth, tears welled in Jade's eyes, threatening her mascara. It felt like she was saying goodbye to Brad in a very significant way, but she knew that it was right. Regardless of everything else, she and Brad were over, and Jade had seen first hand how happy Mandy could make him. She was a kind girl — Jade could see that for sure — and she knew she would enjoy seeing Mandy with a good match.

'I don't think so, Jade,' Mandy sighed, sounding a little hesitant. 'It's far too early, but I appreciate that you said that ... just in case things progress, if you see what I mean.'

'And I did mean what I said, back at the office. We must meet up for a drink and a chat in the New Year.'

'Too right! I want to know what happens with Carl!'

Jade laughed and they said their goodbyes, Jade sensing the beginnings of a friendship that she'd hoped for in the past but never quite found. She had the feeling that Mandy was someone who would be there for her when things in Jade's own life got a bit tough. Men would always be just another complication, but she'd said that she would go and face Carl so she pulled on her coat again and grabbed the keys from on top of the beanbag.

When she reached the car, the temperature had dropped even further than it had earlier, so she ran back to the house for some gloves.

The roads were empty and she reached Montecute in no time at all. Parked outside Carl's place, Jade could see the lights were on in the downstairs flat so he was in. Nervously, she locked up the car and went round to his front door, her heart pounding at a gallop when she suddenly realised the possibility of Carl being inside with somebody else.

18

The whole of the street could hear the clang of the doorbell, Jade was sure. It echoed in the relative silence and she waited, stepping from one foot to another, blowing warm air into her gloves. She never minded the long winter nights and the cosiness they provided, but she never did manage too well with the cold. She continued to wait for Carl's answer but there was no repy.

Jade determined to ring again once and, if there was still no reply, she would climb quickly into her little Corsa and go home. She opened the letterbox briefly as she thought she could hear music filtering through the front door, and was shocked to find it open when her hand was still holding the flap.

'Oh!'

The music grew louder. She'd been right but that didn't help her excruciating embarrassment. She straightened, hoping the late hour at least partially hid the redness on her cheeks.

'Jade? This is a surprise. Do you want to come in?'

Jade tried to subtly peer round the door, wondering if he would have invited her if he already had a visitor, but of course she could see very little.

'Well, so long as it isn't inconvenient,' she said as she went in. She groaned inwardly. Here they were speaking like people out of a Jane Austen novel when they had been kissing with unbridled passion the previous night. Nevertheless, she stepped in demurely, and allowed Carl to take her coat.

'Would you like a drink?' he offered.

Jade shook her head. 'I'm driving. A coffee would be nice, though — I need warming up.'

Despite the civility of the conversation, Carl raised an eyebrow, a smile playing on his lips.

'Coming right up,' he assured, without comment, and Jade's blush deepened, but she couldn't allow herself to be drawn into suggestiveness and driven off track, so she slipped off her gloves and placed them on the kitchen counter, avoiding his gaze as she did so.

'So, nice as it is that you've come over, I am rather surprised. You weren't talking to me in the office. Don't get me wrong, you've made my Christmas by turning up on the doorstep — '

'Don't get carried away, Carl,' Jade interrupted. 'We're not taking up where we left off.' She watched him buzz around the kitchen, getting cups and spooning in the coffee. Proper coffee, she thought with joy, none of that decaf stuff that Brad had. She always kept a sneaky sandwich bag full of her own in her handbag and used that when he wasn't looking.

Or she used to, she thought, with a sigh.

'You ok?' Carl looked at her, not

hiding his concern. 'It's not Dan, is it?' he said, as if it had suddenly dawned on him, but again Jade shook her head.

As she watched him moving around, she noticed the trademark shirt, but this time he wore a sweater on top and jeans instead of chinos. The kitchen was fairly warm but not enough to spend too long in shirtsleeves and she wished she'd worn another layer herself. Tonight, she'd forgotten her nan's advice, but she needn't have worried. When Carl led her into the lounge, flames were licking up the inside of the fireplace and the room was bathed in a gentle glow.

'That's a fire and a half!'

It even overshadowed the beauty of the tree, suffused with lights near the window. Jade waited for Carl to indicate where she should sit but he said nothing, sitting down on the settee. The armchair was covered in photography paper and prints so she had no choice but to seat herself at the opposite end to Carl, memories of a few nights earlier crowding her thoughts, spurring her pulse into overdrive.

Jade smoothed her pencil skirt neatly beneath her, attempting to block out how she'd been feeling when last she had been here. She would stay firmly focused on the present, she determined, reaching nervously to mess with her hair. Of course, she had pinned it up in a bun earlier that evening when meeting Brad. *Was it really only a few hours ago?* she wondered, amazed by the events that had overtaken her.

Carl was looking across at her and she took a tentative sip of her coffee to avoid looking back at him.

'You were right about the photograph for Dan,' she offered at last, beginning to feel uncomfortable. 'The one you suggested was right.'

'Good.'

Carl continued to look at her as Jade searched for something else neutral to say. Nothing sprang to mind and they sat in silence for a while, the fire crackling into the quietness. Jade hadn't realised how tired she had become until the heat began making her feel heavy, but whenever she came back to why she was there, the adrenalin woke her back up.

'That top suits you,' Carl eventually commented, putting his drink down to pull off his sweater and, as it rose, so did his shirt and Jade caught a glimpse of his stomach, remembering its firmness under her hands.

Carl slung the sweater over the arm of the settee beside him and pulled his shirt back down. 'It matches the green of your eyes,' he went on, apparently unaware of the effect he may have had on her. 'You should wear it at work.'

'What's the point,' Jade asked, wryly, 'if the guy who likes it is seeing somebody else?'

'Brad's seeing someone else?' Carl's frown revealed his confusion and he rubbed at his ear. 'Not that Sara Maxwell? She's a dangerous son of a — '

'Not Brad, Carl. You.'

'I'm seeing somebody else? Am I?

Who told you that?'

Carl's eyes glistened with amusement but soon became serious again when he realised Jade wasn't joking.

'No-one told me, Carl. I heard you the other night, on the phone, when I was here.' Nervously, Jade rose and wandered towards the fireplace, wringing her hands, then turned back, knowing she needed to see his response.

'What — Anne?' Carl's voice was incredulous and Jade could see he was truly astounded. Perhaps she had got it all wrong? 'Anne's not a girlfriend, Jade. She's part of a group I run. She needed some reassurance, that's all.'

'Group?'

'A support group.' Carl's demeanour changed in an instant, as if he feared that he'd said too much.

'What sort of support group?' Jade was pressing him hard and in one way she felt quite uncomfortable. It wasn't her business, but it was important to what could happen next. It felt like something she needed to know. 'Carl, you always seem like you're hiding something. The way you backed off when I was here . . . then the phone call . . . '

'It's a support group for some of us who were in hospital together.' Carl's tone was edged with defeat. 'We helped each other stay afloat when things were tough and we decided to keep in touch when we were discharged. We're scattered throughout the country, but Anne lives in Wincanton. She has a husband and four kids.'

'You said she was beautiful . . . ' Jade said quietly.

'She was burned facially,' Carl replied. 'She gets down about her appearance.'

Jade recalled one of the photos on Carl's studio wall in the next room and felt a rush of guilt at her relief on the back of some other woman's misfortune . . . but to know that the call was completely innocent was so much more than she'd hoped. At best, she'd thought it might be an ex who wouldn't let go.

'And you . . . ?' Jade's heart was in her mouth and the words edged themselves out around it. Was she about to push him too far?

'I was burned on my back. Caught a bomb blast and didn't run fast enough. At least I was facing the other way.'

'So that's why you wouldn't take your shirt off?' Jade's tone softened and she lowered herself onto the arm of the settee.

'It's hilarious, isn't it?' Carl's laugh was far from convincing. 'I spend my time encouraging others to accept themselves as they are but I can't face my own scars. What a hypocrite.'

He picked up his coffee cup and drained it as Jade digested his words. She knew she needed to find the right ones to respond with. It would matter to Carl and he would remember them after a moment like this.

'Perhaps encouraging others' acceptance is a way of moving towards your own?' She sat silently for a while, wanting to embrace him but feeling the moment wasn't right. 'Do you honestly think that scars would make any difference to me?' she finally asked, then wished that she could retract it. Of course he thought that she'd care or he wouldn't have run from her like he had.

'It's not just the scars, though. I have a tattoo over my back,' he told her, apparently in way of an explanation. 'It was my pride and joy when I was a soldier. Now it's just an unholy mess.'

'But it's your mess,' Jade whispered, moving down onto the settee and shuffling along next to him. Her hand rested on his, touching his leg. 'And if it was your mess, I would adore it. Would you honestly let it get in the way of your happiness when it's obviously already stolen so much?'

'But why me when you've got the perfect Bradley Wilson?'

Jade laughed aloud. 'He might be perfect to look at, but I can assure you he has his flaws. As have we all . . . '

The last line dwindled into silence as the reality of her own future flew up and hit her. In the end, Brad couldn't accept her and her uncertain future, so why should the man next to her now? She looked at Carl who was watching her quizzically.

'So, what's your Achilles heel, Jade Cooke? Why aren't you perfect?' he asked.

Jade heaved a sigh, relaxing back into the cushions behind her. She felt Carl's hand turn under her own and give hers a small, gentle squeeze.

'Well, as it's time for confessions . . . Dan has Duchenne Muscular Dystrophy, as you know, and although I haven't got it myself, I have . . .'

'A fifty-fifty chance of being a carrier. I know, Jade. I looked up his illness when you first told me. I promise you I wasn't snooping about your own prognosis — I just wanted to know what you were dealing with. Besides, there's such thing as fostering or adoption, you know.' Carl's Irish lilt reassured her, his thumb gently stroking the back of her hand. 'Not that I'm jumping the gun or anything . . . '

The cheekiness of his wink cracked her mouth into a smile. His hand moved from her own and he lifted it over her head and pulled her into him, kissing her hair. It wasn't the type of kiss that she was used to receiving from Brad. Carl's lips lingered and she could feel him inhaling her scent, almost drawing her in by osmosis. The heat of the room was making her drowsy and she closed her eyes and breathed deeply, his familiar musky aftershave making her feel as if she was home. She seemed to fit perfectly into the shape of him and she snuggled closer, wishing she could stay here forever. Carl had a way of making her problems seem surmountable . . . sometimes even small.

'I guess that's why you don't swim now,' she said fuzzily, feeling the movement of his body as he nodded his reply.

The past week had completely exhausted her, making everything seem such an effort and she felt that at last she had found her sanctuary. It was time to tell him, Jade realised. The weight of him as he rested his chin on her head was the most welcome burden she'd ever felt.

'I'm not with Brad any more,' she announced plainly. 'We finished this evening. He's gone to Bristol to spend Christmas Day with his parents.'

In an instant, Carl was gone.

He withdrew his arm from around her, the weight of him leaving her and, horrified that she had misread the situation, Jade straightened on the settee, not wanting to face him, not wanting to have him run from her again. Despite the heat from the fireplace, she felt a sudden chill as his body moved completely away from her and his shadow fell over the room as he got to his feet.

Panic almost strangled her. What on earth had she done? Carl was pacing the floor, his shadow roving with him, until finally he stopped and crouched down on his haunches in front of her.

His features were even more striking as the firelight danced upon them and it was all Jade could do to not reach out and touch his shadowy cheek with her palm; but she held back, not wanting to make everything worse. Surely she couldn't be blown out twice in one week by the same man?

'Jade, what are you saying? Are you saying what I've been hoping for nearly three years, 'cos if you are and we do this, it can't just be a rebound. I won't do this if you just fancy a bit of ex-army. For me to be, well . . . intimate, it has to be . . .'

Jade felt the rage build in her chest. Aware that she had him off guard and at a disadvantage, she pushed him gently so that he lost his balance and toppled against the coffee table behind him. He roared as he fell backwards, his pride appearing more hurt more than his body. Jade barely stifled a giggle.

'Serves you right!' she said primly, watching him flounder. 'Fancy a bit of ex-army? What sort of girl do you think I am?'

'What sort of girl do I think you are?'

He scrambled back to his feet, this time moving even closer, his face just inches from hers and his eyes intense. 'If you really want to know, then I'll tell you! I think that you're the girl I've always been looking for. I think you're the girl I've watched from nearby, not afar, for almost three years. You, Jade, are the answer to my dreams — and to my nightmares, no doubt.'

He finished his soliloquy with a grin and she knew then that she was irretrievably lost, never to return from the gentle brown trap of his eyes.

'But, just to make sure, shall we find out?' He held out a hand and she took it, letting him pull her to her feet. 'I don't suppose you're wearing your Santa gift?' he teased her with a wink, and Jade winked back with a smile.

'Funny you should say that . . . ' she said, letting him lead her down the hall.

19

'I wonder if you'd have a problem with turning the light out. Just this first time?'

Jade looked up in surprise. Carl was messing about with the duvet, pulling it back then straightening it up again, quite obviously ill at ease.

She walked around the bed and put her arms around him. 'Are you sure you want to do this?' she asked, as sensitively as she could manage. 'There's no rush. We've plenty of time . . . '

Carl interjected before she had the chance to finish. 'No rush?' His laugh rumbled through his body, his muscles tightening against her. 'I wouldn't call this rushing. I've been waiting for this since we first met three years ago!'

'Point taken.' She laughed. 'I was just saying . . . ' Jade ran a hand through his hair, at last discovering that it was as soft as she'd imagined it would be and she did it again.

'Hey. That's my look you're messing with, Miss Cooke. No-one does that without paying,' and with one twist, Carl had Jade pinned on the bed.

'That was impressive!' she laughed. 'What else can you wow me with?'

Carl pulled himself up to his full six feet height. 'I wouldn't know where to start,' he replied, with a nonchalant shrug. 'You'll just have to wait and see.'

Seeing might be a problem, however, Jade thought to herself, if he wanted to turn out the light. She wanted to see him, she wanted to see every inch of Carl Heaney. She reached up and pulled him down to her, undoing a couple of his shirt buttons and, as predicted, she felt him start to tense up.

'It's ok,' she reassured him. 'I won't do anything you don't want me to. I just want to feel you against me.'

At first she teased him, as he'd teased her in Kev's hall at the party, brushing her lips against his, but it didn't last long. Carl didn't seem in the mood for messing about this time and he kissed her full on the mouth, one hand under her neck, pulling her closer. He tasted delicious and she melted against him, delighting in his response as his kiss grew firmer. His lips trailed a line down her neck to her chest, his fingertips brushing her skin as he undid the buttons on her top.

'It really does suit you,' he said smiling, 'but we don't really need it right now.'

Jade lifted her body and he removed it, letting out a low whistle. 'It fits you a treat!'

'You should see the rest of the set,' Jade suggested, discovering he didn't need telling twice. Ten seconds later, her skirt had joined the emerald blouse lying messily on the floor.

'You're even more beautiful than my fantasies,' he confessed, softly. 'And I can assure you, when it comes to you, I've had a lot.'

Jade's pulse tipped into overdrive as Carl's hands ran over her body, tracing her contours, but the next moment, he reached over to the light switch, ready to plunge them both into darkness and Jade had to think fast. She didn't want it to be like this.

'Wait, Carl, wait. Get out one of your ties.'

'What? Jade, stop messing about. I don't think I can wait much longer . . . '

'I'm not messing about, Carl. Get a tie.'

Heaving a sigh of frustration, Carl walked across to the wardrobe by the window and pulled a blue tie from the rack on the inside of the door. She watched the flap of his open shirt as he moved, exposing the dark hair beneath his navel, tantalising with its promise of what was to come.

'Here,' he said, failing to hide the impatience in his voice as he dropped the tie on the bed. 'What do you want to do now? Tie me to the bedpost so that I can't run away again?'

His laugh was half-hearted and Jade chose not to join in.

'Blindfold me. Turn off the overhead light and put on the bedside one. Then you can still see me.'

Jade turned her back on him and waited as Carl carefully placed the thickest part of the tie over her eyes and tied it at the back of her head.

'Is that ok? Not too tight?' Carl's hands dropped to her shoulders, resting there for a while before stroking down her arms to her wrists. Jade felt him take hold of her hand and place it on the belt below his navel and she took the cue, fumbling around for a moment then using the other hand too. Finally, it loosened and she felt the weight of the jeans disappear as they dropped heavily to the floor. All of a sudden, Carl was gone, then she heard the click of the overhead light and the quieter click of the bedside lamp. The change in brightness was detectible through the tie, but she could identify nothing else.

Starting at his feet, Jade's hands slid up and over the muscles of his calves, the hairs on his legs soft beneath her palms. Together, her hands formed a circle and embraced one of Carl's legs above the knee, travelling up in an ever-widening ring until they could no longer touch together, such was his thighs' muscular bulk.

'You do work out, don't you?' she murmured between kisses, and Carl's heart beat loudly close to her ear and she listened to the proof of his excitement, glorying in how it raced.

'I have weights,' he sighed, and Jade pinned down his arms so that he would lie still. His arms were far stronger than hers but she sensed that he chose to give her the power as she straddled him, bending closer to his neck. She inhaled deeply, nudging his shirt collar out of the way, the musky scent that she loved deepening the eroticism she felt, and she breathed deeply again, wishing she could somehow inhale him into her body. She lowered herself so that her bra brushed his chest, her mouth planting minute kisses on his neck, his ear, his hair. Sitting upright once more, she

286

ran her fingers through his hair, the tips massaging his scalp and she felt his torso relax as the tension drained out of him.

She needed Carl to relax, yet still be so desperate for her that he couldn't care less what she saw or felt.

In one smooth movement, Jade felt for Carl's shoulder and encouraged him over onto his stomach. His change of position was hesitant but more decisive than she'd dared hope. He allowed her to slip his shirt down over his arms and right off.

'Jade . . . '

'Sshh,' she whispered softly.

Her hand felt for his shoulder and she placed a hand either side of his neck, massaging again to relax him, her thumb rubbing a firm circle at the nape. She could hear his breathing deepen and slow, becoming more tranquil, so she carried on until she sensed it was safe to move on.

Moving on meant making contact with Carl's back. She guessed no-one had ever touched him there since the bomb blast and the weight of responsibility lay on her like a ten ton rock. She bore it as best she could, steadying herself as inconspicuously as possible, letting her palms drop from Carl's neck and descend to his shoulder blades.

At once, she felt changes in his skin as her fingertips trailed slowly down his back. Some parts were drier and leathery to the touch, but every inch of the skin that she touched was Carl and she found him irresistible.

She wanted to lie down and press the whole of her body against him, but she held back, loath to overstep the mark Carl had laid out. His body tensed under her hand, but as he became accustomed to her touch, she felt the muscles slacken beneath her again.

'A lot of the nerves have been damaged.' His voice whispered into her darkness and she stopped moving to hear. 'I can feel some of what you're doing, but not all.'

'Is it ok?'

His body moved underneath her as he nodded his response.

'More ok than I thought,' he whispered.

Jade felt Carl's body tip and took it as her cue to let him get up, but he didn't. Once she had lifted herself from on top of him, Carl turned his body, pressing her onto the bed. She could map every muscle of his torso as it bore down on her and suddenly his hot breath sighed into her mouth. Although his lips were soft on hers, his kiss grew swiftly harder as his control began to ebb. It was as if something had been released inside him and Jade sensed that, exposing himself to her in that way, Carl had maybe found himself once again.

Jade's head dropped back on the pillows as Carl's mouth began to make its descent, her back arching up towards him.

She returned his kiss fervently and the response was dramatic and instant. Trembling fingers found the clasp between her shoulder blades, expertly releasing it within moments.

He sighed her name as his kisses travelled lower and the smallest stroke of his fingertips sent a rocket of fire through her body and the ache for him that had been in her for longer than she would admit to rose almost into pain. She longed to see his face, share his expressions of pleasure, but she knew she would need to stay in the darkness until Carl was ready to emerge from his own.

For now, she savoured the sensations washing over her, but the pleasure was so exquisite that it almost took her too far.

'No, please,' she breathed, twisting away from him. 'Not yet. I don't want to . . .'

'I think I could actually eat you.'

His words made her smile and she felt the tie tighten above her cheekbones. She could feel Carl draw back and sit up. After some moments, his hands reached around the back of her head, fiddling with the knot of the tie and suddenly the darkness dropped away and Jade was blinking into the relative brightness that dazzled her for a while.

Her focus was off and it was some time before she caught the way Carl was drinking her in and the obvious yearning within him. There was the hint of a smile in his eyes, but his mouth was firm and serious as his gaze travelled over her body.

Totally breathless, she was scorched by a desire she'd never imagined existed and gave in with blissful abandon. This evening, she couldn't wait. Every second seemed to have stretched into forever since Carl had last kissed her at the party, each moment since then torturing her with their emptiness, teasing her with what life could have held.

She tried not to think about what had gone wrong, focusing only on the here and now and the gentle brush of Carl's fingertips as he loosened the bows on her panties. They dropped open, first at one hip then the other, and then there was nothing left of her that wasn't his.

'Carl . . . ' she breathed.

Tonight, for the first time, Jade knew that it wouldn't take much to bring her over the edge, her need for him was so great, she felt she would turn herself inside out to satisfy the desire.

Towering over her, Carl looked for all the world a magnificent army soldier in his prime, every sinew and muscle in his body rippled under his skin.

In the time before he had withdrawn into himself after the blast, he must have attracted girls to him like north and south-seeking poles, Jade realised, but she had him now, or at least she was about to, and he was the man she intended to keep.

She applied a little more pressure with her fingers, drawing a harsh breath from deep within him, and she revelled in her utter control. His breathing became ragged and she knew she was more than doing it right, but suddenly he pulled away and lowered his body gently onto hers.

Yet, instead of moving into her, he pressed himself onto her abdomen, and the heat of him burned her flesh. She lifted herself up towards him once again, willing the contact to be stronger but knowing that, if it was, she wouldn't last.

'I want you,' she urged.

'I bet I want you more,' he moaned, still making her wait.

'Don't tease, Carl,' she pleaded, but before the sentence was finished he was there, stemming any more words she might have said, escalating his need for release and intensifying her own. She wrapped herself around him, drawing him to the hub of her, the emotional, spiritual centre that no-one else had ever quite reached.

His pelvis brushed against her as he moved, drawing her closer to the Armageddon of pleasure, and she curled her calves around his, exposing the nerves that made her dizzy. Carl's rhythm quickened in response, but he was waiting, she knew, although he didn't have to wait too much longer.

The near-unbearable pleasure gathered itself from the depths of her abdomen, building into an ecstasy and shattering her into minuscule pieces until the world around her splintered into oblivion.

'Is . . . tú . . . mo . . . ghrá.'

Carl's answer tore into her and sweat had surfaced on his body. Jade felt the matching dampness on her own, but then she was still alight, her nerves seared by the pleasure pulsing through her. They clung together as one until the last of him was spent and then they clung together some more.

Jade sensed Carl's reluctance to let go was as great as her own when he kissed her on the forehead then on the lips softly, over and over, before the time to retreat finally arrived.

As she felt the desolation of their bodies parting, she remembered his strange words.

'What was that you said, Carl?' Jade

asked quietly, her centre still throbbing from the explosion that had ripped through her entire body.

Carl lay next to her, gazing up at the ceiling.

'Far too soon to tell you,' he breathed, his chest still rising and falling deeply from his exertions. 'You'll see, before long.'

Jade watched him for a while, intrigued by his evasion, then looked at the clock on the bedside cabinet, glowing red in the subtle light.

'Oh look, it's Christmas Day!' she said, amazed at how the evening had flown, yet how much had happened since leaving home for the first time that night.

'Wait here. I'll just be a minute.'

'Carl . . . what are you doing?' Jade laughed.

Carl leapt from the bed, suddenly rejuvenated, despite the energy he'd just expended and Jade knew he had forgotten himself when he left the room without covering up.

Silently, she rejoiced. It would be a

long time before he could be carefree about his body, if ever — she knew that and accepted it — but perhaps one day he might swim with her. Perhaps, one day, he might even let her photograph him with her camera, so that his picture could join his other subjects on the studio wall.

For now, she was thrilled that he could trust her enough to share his body with her.

Carl strode back through the door, an envelope in his hand.

'I didn't wrap it. Didn't do much with it, in fact. To be honest, I wondered if I might never get to give it to you. Here. It's Christmas Day.'

Grabbing his dressing gown hanging behind the door, he threw it to her then pulled on a T-shirt.

'Open it now, but get under the covers or you'll get cold.'

He jumped in beside her, watching her open the envelope like a puppy waiting for its first bone and Jade smiled at his eagerness. He rarely revealed this side of himself at work and she liked it. It made him seem carefree and fun.

'Oh . . . my . . . word . . . are you serious?' Jade stared at the tickets in disbelief, her hand still trembling a little from their lovemaking.

'I've never been anything but serious when it comes to you, Miss Cooke. You might believe me one day.'

'But these are . . . '

'For you and Dan. Disneyland for a week. I spoke to Jenny to make sure you could get the time off.'

Carl plumped up the pillows behind them, making sure Jade was comfortable, but she could have been sitting on a bed of nails and not even noticed.

'I booked you one of those themed rooms in the park. I hope he's not too old but I remember you once saying he loved Disney movies. I thought April would be good. Not too long to wait, but the weather will be warmer for him.'

'No-one's ever too old for Disney . . . ' Jade's voice trailed off as tears threatened behind her eyes, but they weren't the type of tears she had shed earlier in the evening. These were tears of elated disbelief.

'I just can't believe that you would have thought of this.' She paused for a moment, looking into the eyes that she hoped would gaze at her that way forever. 'I wish you were coming too.'

'Let's see what Dan thinks of me, first!' Carl laughed, planting a lingering kiss on her cheek. 'I'd love to come, if he's up for it. We've got plenty of time to decide.'

'I just can't believe it,' Jade repeated. 'How did you find something that was just so right?'

'I usually do.' Carl winked mysteriously, nodding towards the pink and black garments discarded on the floor.

'Ah well, I did sort of work that one out, after a while.'

'And haven't you found the odd gift on your desk over the past year or so?'

'My very own Secret Santa,' she giggled. 'And to think that for ages I thought it was Brad.'

'Ah, c'mon,' he said in his beautifully lilting Irish accent and grinned, leaning back in mock model-mode. 'It had to be someone with style.'

A text message tone buzzed into the seclusion of Carl's room and Jade reached down for it in the mess of her clothes on the floor. She slid open the lock and read the message with surprise, having expected it to be from her mum.

Brad texted me. Looks like it's going to be a Bristonian Christmas Day for me after all!:-)

Jade quickly sent a smiley face back.

'Looks like Mandy's all sorted for tomorrow,' she said, pleased that Mandy wouldn't be spending it all alone.

She showed Carl the text and, when he'd read it, she looked him straight in the eye.

'So, what are you doing tomorrow, then? I want to show you off to Mum and Dan — seeing as you apparently have so much style!' She laughed, feeling carefree for the first time in ages.

'What . . . ? Well, I was . . . '

'We're eating at The Oak. It'll be more fun for Dan with another guy around. You could give him your present yourself! The table's all booked and there's a space now, obviously.'

Jade instantly clapped a hand over her mouth.

'What's up?' Dan took her hand.

'I'm sorry.' Jade avoided his gaze. 'That was so insensitive. About the spare place at the table and of course you must have plans. Forget I said anything. It's just . . . '

'I'll come. Just try and stop me! I was supposed to be seeing my parents but they'll be made-up to know where I'll be. They know all about you.'

Jade stared at him in surprise. 'They do?'

'Fed up with hearing about you, in fact.'

Jade laughed, but her laughter didn't last long. She knew she'd never get bored with hearing his beautiful Irish lilt, but for now she was happy enough that Carl's mouth was put to another use.

As the kiss went on, and on, and on for the start of a lifetime, Jade was sure she could hear the words of a Christmas song filtering through the open window behind Carl's curtains. It sounded familiar and she listened hard, eyes closed as Carl's passion devoured her.

''Tis the season to be jolly . . . tra la la la la la la la.'

This time, Jade very definitely did feel jolly. Instead of tuning it out, she gave herself up to a particularly romantic yuletide celebration as her heart silently sang along inside.

THE END

We do hope that you have enjoyed reading this large print book.

Did you know that all of our titles are available for purchase?

We publish a wide range of high quality large print books including:
Romances, Mysteries, Classics
General Fiction
Non Fiction and Westerns

Special interest titles available in large print are:
The Little Oxford Dictionary
Music Book, Song Book
Hymn Book, Service Book

Also available from us courtesy of Oxford University Press:
Young Readers' Dictionary
(large print edition)
Young Readers' Thesaurus
(large print edition)

For further information or a free brochure, please contact us at:
Ulverscroft Large Print Books Ltd.,
The Green, Bradgate Road, Anstey,
Leicester, LE7 7FU, England.
Tel: (00 44) **0116 236 4325**
Fax: (00 44) **0116 234 0205**

Other titles in the
Linford Romance Library:

FLAMES THAT MELT

Angela Britnell

Tish Carlisle returns from Tennessee to clear out her late father's house in Cornwall — to several surprises. The first is the woman and baby she discovers living there and the second is her father's solicitor, Nico De Burgh, who was Tish's first love. Nico fights their renewed attraction because of a promise made to his foster father but Tish won't give up on him. They must share their secrets before they have any chance of a loving future together . . .

TENDER TAKEOVER

Susan Udy

To Sandy's dismay, she finds herself working for Oliver Carlton, the charismatic man who single-handedly destroyed her family — so when her hatred threatens to turn into something dangerously close to attraction, she uses all of her willpower to fight it. However, it swiftly becomes apparent that Oliver has romantic interests elsewhere, when Sandy catches sight of him with his arm around another woman . . .

HIDDEN HEARTACHE

Suzanna Ross

Doctor Emma Bradshaw's life is disrupted when Nick Rudd arrives back in town to take up a post at the GP practice where she works. It's not so easy to ignore the love of your life when you have to see him every day, but Emma is keeping her distance — Nick let her down badly in the past. Now, though, he'll do anything to rekindle the trust and love she once showed him . . .

MISTRESS OF SEABROOK

Phyllis Mallett

When her exiled father dies, Victoria comes to England from her native America to clear his name, but things go wrong from the outset. She meets her unscrupulous uncle, Landers Radbourne, and his hateful family, and begins to realise what an impossible task she has taken on. Greed and jealousy lead to a murderous climax, putting Victoria's very life in jeopardy . . .